# NO LOVE LIKE NANTUCKET

---

## A SWEET ISLAND INN NOVEL (BOOK FOUR)

### GRACE PALMER

# JOIN MY MAILING LIST!

Click the link below to join my mailing list and receive updates, freebies, release announcements, and more!

JOIN HERE:

https://readerlinks.com/l/1060002

# ALSO BY GRACE PALMER

# NO LOVE LIKE NANTUCKET

**She built the Sweet Island Inn. But can Toni Benson build a life of happiness for herself?**

Toni Benson's life has been a roller coaster.

Years ago, the heartbreak caused by a cheating ex-husband left her in tatters.

Then she discovered the rundown fixer-upper that would become the Sweet Island Inn.

For a while, things were good.

But when her brother Henry's tragic death sends her reeling all over again, she's back to square one.

So she sets off on an overseas journey, in hopes of learning from scratch what kind of woman she is meant to be.

She isn't looking for love.

But it finds her anyway.

Follow Toni's journey as the Nantucket native navigates an explosive romance, an unbearable tragedy, and the prospect of starting life anew in her late fifties.

In the end, only one thing is certain: there is no love like her love for Nantucket.

～

*Travel back to the very beginnings of the Sweet Island Inn and follow along with the soaring highs and heartbreaking lows of Aunt Toni's story in NO LOVE LIKE NANTUCKET, the fourth installment of author Grace Palmer's beloved Sweet Island Inn series.*

# 1

ATLANTA, GEORGIA—JUNE 15, 2000

Looking back, it was easy to see that this was the kind of day that would change her life forever.

But at the time, it seemed to Toni Benson like it was just any other day. Just a normal Thursday in the middle of June, two weeks shy of her ninth wedding anniversary to Jared. The sun was shining; the birds were chirping; not a thing looked out of place.

Work that day went by in a flash. She spent most of it thinking about the surprise she was planning for her husband and browsing the internet to double-check all the reservations she had made.

She'd never been much good at keeping secrets, especially not from Jared. He was the more mysterious of the two of them, certainly. As a matter of fact, in twelve years together, she'd hardly learned much about him at all.

He always said, with the same sort of exasperated, *Why are you even bothering with this?* kind of tone, that there just wasn't much to know. He had a mother he didn't talk to and a hometown not worth mentioning. No father figure, no siblings, no past to speak of.

If Toni pressed him on it—when she'd had a glass of wine, say, or if she was just feeling a little nosy—he'd mention something vague about small-town life. He'd been born in either Kansas or Arkansas —she never could remember which—and then, according to his version of events, he'd more or less shown up one day at the law firm where Toni worked as a paralegal. She remembered he was toting both a charming smile and an impressive binder with which to pitch the firm's partners on his budding software company.

That was that, as far as origin stories go. Jared had stayed behind after his presentation to flirt with Toni a bit, while she made excuses to linger and help him take down the backdrop he'd set up for his presentation. Neither of them had been in any great hurry to leave.

Eventually, he'd asked to take her to dinner, and she'd pretended to ponder it for a bit before saying yes. He was awfully handsome, which made her a bit wary, but he seemed genuine enough. He had dimples set on either side of a country boy's *aw-shucks* kind of smile, and that felt like something that could be relied upon.

One date led to another, and before Toni knew it, they were moving in together into a house in Virginia Highlands, an up-and-coming neighborhood near Atlanta.

It was fun for the longest time. Jared loved to take Toni on weekend drives in his Mazda convertible around the rich neighborhoods in Cobb County. They'd slow down or stop outside the gates of the truly jaw-dropping mansions to ogle. He would whistle and slap Toni on the thigh to point out this ironwork fountain or that fluted marble column, which always made her laugh.

Jared was like a little kid on those excursions, just excited to see parts of the world that blew his hair back. And if he seemed a little overly keen on the trappings of the rich folks—well, who could blame him? They were awfully nice houses, after all. Anybody would get a little bit jealous, standing outside the gates of homes like that.

His excitement made Toni excited about life, too. He could be such an infectious, spontaneous guy, the kind who shows up late to dinner and immediately orders three bottles of wine for the table. Not because he was rich, though his software company had at long last begun to show some real promise in that department. But because it was simply a fun thing to do.

Which was why she was thrilled and nervous alike to be the one taking the lead in the "fun and spontaneous" category for their Fourth of July plans.

"You think he'll like this one, Solange?" she asked nervously. Her fellow paralegal, Solange—a gorgeous woman with skin like caramel and perfect, voluminous ringlets that Toni, with her stick-straight blonde hair, was eternally jealous of—looked over to Toni's computer screen for the umpteenth time that day.

"Stop," Solange counseled patiently. "You're freaking out. He's gonna love it. He loves you. You love him. What else matters?"

Toni bit her lip. "Everything matters, Sol. I want this to be fun. And you know Jared. He can be, I don't know...particular, sometimes."

That was true, too. For every memory of fun, life-of-the-party Jared she had, there was an equal and opposite memory of a time when he just hadn't reacted the way she thought he would to something.

The last time she'd tried to surprise him was at his thirty-fifth birthday party four years ago. She'd promised him a quiet, candlelit evening with just the two of them at a restaurant. But when they showed up to the dinner spot, his friends and coworkers came out of the woodwork to hoot and holler, "Surprise!"

She thought he'd laugh. She did so love his laugh.

Jared hadn't laughed, though. Not even a little bit. Instead, he'd stood stock-still in the middle of everyone for one impossibly long moment with his jaw and fists clenched before storming out of the restaurant steaming mad.

He wouldn't even look at her for a while after she followed him out into the night and tried to figure out what on earth was going on in his brain.

"I just don't like surprises," he growled again and again through gritted teeth, as if that explained anything whatsoever.

He seemed like he was terribly close to making Toni send everyone home. But at the last second, he'd relented and gone back inside. After reluctantly shaking everyone's hands and doing his rounds, he'd corralled a drink and nursed it by himself in the corner until it was time to go.

Toni didn't plan any surprises for a long, long while after that.

But for reasons she wasn't quite prepared to confront at the moment, it had begun to feel important to her over the last couple months to do something big and dramatic in her marriage.

She wished she knew why. If she'd had something she could point to, a specific instance or conversation or something along those lines, she might feel better about this plan she was conjuring up. But, as frustrating as it was, she didn't have anything of the sort. All she had was a vague feeling that she ought to do *something*.

She'd tried to bring her concerns up to Solange or to her sister-in-law Mae or one of her other close friends at least half a dozen times since she'd first noticed the little thread of anxiety unspooling itself in the pit of her stomach. But every time she tried to muster up the words, she fell silent before she could spit it out. It just sounded silly, shrewish, insignificant.

*Something's wrong in my marriage.*

*Like what?* They would inevitably ask her. *Did he cheat? Did he lie? Did he hurt you?*

*No, no, no, nothing of the sort. I can't say, exactly, can't quite put my finger on it. But I just know it's something.*

If it sounded silly when she practiced that little exchange in her bathroom mirror, it would certainly sound worse in a conversation with one of her friends.

And if it sounded absurd with one of her friends—well, then, Jared was likely to just roll his eyes and stomp out of the house rather than engage with it for even a fraction of a second. He didn't have the patience for anything that wasn't concrete, that he couldn't put his hands on.

The disquiet grew over time as she ignored it. So after she'd decided that she had to do something, the question then became, what kind of something?

And then, one day, the solution had presented itself. They needed some time to recharge and reconnect, she and Jared. A weekend away on Lake Lanier would be just the ticket. They could celebrate the Fourth of July, their ninth anniversary, and their love all at once. Three birds with one stone. Problems solved, presto change-o, cue the happily ever after.

It seemed like a neat answer to their unspecified problems. And besides, Jared had mentioned from time to time over the years that he wanted a boat. Toni figured that he'd get a kick out of renting one and captaining it out from the dock attached to their cabin. Truth be told, she quite liked the thought of a shirtless, suntanned Jared issuing nautical orders.

So she'd dived in headfirst with the planning. When Toni Benson put her mind to something, she did it thoroughly. It was part of why she was so good at her job. Working in a law firm, especially with the high-powered, *"I want that document on my desk by yesterday!"* types who owned the practice that employed her, meant never missing a step.

She hadn't grown up wanting to be a paralegal. But it suited her in its own stiff, paper-shuffling sort of way. There was a part of her soul that sang when all the numbers in the spreadsheets tied out, or when she could clear the stacks of paper from her desk at the end of a satisfying workday and say, "Ahhh, all done."

She didn't need romance in her workplace. She had that at home. Or rather, she used to. And after she and Jared had their weekend away, wrapped up in each other, she'd have it back again in spades.

"Show me again, then, honey," Solange said. She was a wonderfully patient woman, thoughtful and kind.

"You're the best," Toni murmured. She turned to her screen and started clicking through the photos one by one.

The cabin on the shore that she'd chosen really was gorgeous. The first picture showed a long wooden dock that reached out like a finger to stroke the surface of the lake. The water around it was still, smooth, and so blue that it made her eyes hurt. She was already savoring the thought of unwinding out there in the evening, sipping a glass of wine as the sun set over the trees in the distance.

The rest of the house was just as cute. It was one of those homes built to coax its residents out onto the wraparound porch whenever possible. Half of the porch was screened in and festooned with fans to keep beating at the lazy summer air while someone snoozed in the hammock or one of the big, cozy rocking chairs. The other part was open to the breeze. Tasteful red cloth upholstery tied together all of the patio furniture.

Indoors was rustic and snug. Blond wooden beams held up the ceiling, the stairs, the mantelpiece, and the railings that lined the walkways between upstairs bedrooms. She loved how the light of the homey, DIY mason jar lamps in the kitchen added a warm shimmer to the wooden cabinetry.

And the master bedroom upstairs, with its massive French double doors, opened right up onto a second intimate porch holding another pair of rocking chairs that practically had "Jared" and "Toni" written on them already.

"If he doesn't like that, then you're gonna have to throw the man out," Solange said wryly.

Toni laughed, maybe a little louder than she intended to. She glimpsed Rogelio, one of the sterner partners, glance up in irritation from his corner office.

"Just tell me one more time that he'll love it."

"Honey," Solange said, resting a comforting hand on Toni's forearm. "He's going to love it. Just ease up. Have a fun weekend. Drink some wine, smooch your hubby, watch the sunset. You're gonna have fun, okay, doll?"

When she said it like that, there was no room for disagreement. Toni smiled. This time, she meant it.

A little while later, it was finally quitting time, thank the Lord. Toni swept her things into her bag, turned off her computer, and spent a minute making sure that everything was neatly organized so she could start tomorrow with a clean slate.

She was just about to turn and head for her car in the parking lot when Rogelio strode up to her desk and announced his arrival with a rap of his knuckles.

"Hi, Rog," Toni said with a smile. "You need anything from me? I was just about to head out."

Rogelio was a tall, tanned man from the Philippines with a shiny bald spot and big hands that were constantly in motion. He had a way of talking, sort of stern and borderline angry, that some of the other paralegals found intimidating. But his mannerisms had never bothered Toni. He just liked work to be done right, and she liked doing it right. In fact, they got along fairly well.

"Did you get the deposition transcripts from the Martinelli trial finished?"

"The coroner's or the husband's?"

"Husband's."

She nodded. "In your in-box already. The coroner's, too, actually," she added with a wink.

"Did you set up the admin hearing for the Gantt Co. case?"

"July 17, 4 p.m."

"Did you—"

"Dr. Tompkins from Georgia Tech will be providing expert testimony on the blood spatters, the latest draft of the motion for retrial is uploaded to the firm's cloud, and I sent the appendices for the two memos in the Buchanan thing over to Desiree to approve."

Rogelio, for a change, was actually smiling by the time Toni was done listing off all the tasks that she'd already squared away.

"You know, sometimes I don't know why I even bother to ask. You are always on top of things. What would we do without you, Toni?" he mused playfully.

She laughed. "You'd find a way."

"I'm not so sure we would."

"Need anything else from me before I head out?"

"No, no," he said, waving a hand in a fatherly sort of way at her. "Go home. Tell Jared I said hello."

"Will do. Have a good night, Rogelio. G'night, Solange!"

She waved goodbye to everyone as she looped her purse over her shoulder and strode out into the early evening sun.

Atlanta traffic being what it was, the drive home was agonizingly long. But that was all right with Toni. She usually did her best thinking on her commute to and from work. Something about the warm silence of the car and the sun rising or setting over the downtown skyscrapers always kept the wheels in her head turning nicely.

She spent the first fifteen minutes going over and over the plan for the lake house. They would get there on Sunday, two days before the Fourth, so they could unpack, unwind, and make a quick run to the grocery store to pick up food and wine for the remainder of their vacation.

She had a menu planned already—seared scallops with endive and radicchio, which would pair perfectly with the buttery, oaky chardonnay she had in mind—and smiled at the thought of strolling down the dock after dinner, hand in hand with Jared, to watch the boaters heading home in the dying evening light.

Just then, her cell phone started to buzz in her purse. She fished it out and smiled even bigger when she saw who was calling.

"Mae, dear! How are you?"

"Up to my eyeballs in stuff to do, as always," Mae replied, though Toni could hear the hint of a smile on the edge of her voice.

"You wouldn't have it any other way," Toni said with a laugh.

"No, of course not. But I reserve the right to complain."

"Hey," Toni said, "you're the one who chose to marry my brother. I could've told you that he wouldn't exactly be fumbling all over himself to help you with the household stuff."

Mae laughed at that. "Oh God, no, I don't let him anywhere near the chores. Last time I told him to do the dishes, he scrubbed all the finish off my best cast iron skillet. I darn near made him sleep in the doghouse for the night."

"Head in the clouds, that one," Toni agreed. "How're the kids?"

"Let's see. Give me one sec, I just have to remember their names..."

Toni chuckled. "How you manage four of them is beyond me. Especially a little terror on wheels like your youngest."

"Brent is a devil with an angel's smile," Mae agreed. "It amazes me to this day how quick he took to running. He crawled for all of three steps before he decided it wasn't fast enough for him. Come to think of it, Sara was much the same."

"The two of them have a lot of fire. It's a good thing your older ones balance them out a bit."

"That they do," Mae said. "Although that's hard in its own way. Eliza is fourteen, and she is certainly proving that everything folks say about teenage girls is true."

Toni furrowed her brow. "Have you two been butting heads?"

"No, not quite. She's so...inwardly focused, I suppose. Does very well at school, so it's not that. Does well at everything, actually. But she keeps things quite close to the chest. I just worry about her, is all."

"That's your job, hon. But Eliza is a smart cookie. She'll be just fine. I have no doubt about that."

"Of course, of course."

"And Holly?"

"Sweet as molasses. Loves her momma, loves her daddy, loves her siblings, loves her life."

Toni grinned. "Truer words have never been spoken. That one is heaven-sent." She could hear the clatter of plates in the background. Mae must be making dinner. "What're you serving up tonight?"

"I'm tired, so I took the easy way out and made meatloaf," Mae said absentmindedly.

Toni rolled her eyes. "I know darn well what that means, Mae. You aren't fooling anyone. You've probably been in the kitchen all afternoon, sculpting a meatloaf made by the angels."

"Shush," Mae scolded playfully, "you don't know that."

"Somehow, I think I hit the nail on the head."

"Well, anyway," said Mae with a laugh, changing the subject, "the reason I was calling in the first place was because Henry told me you had news about the Fourth. Are you and Jared still coming up?"

"Oh!" Toni exclaimed, feeling suddenly guilty. "That blockhead didn't fill you in? Lord, I could bop him sometimes. I'm so sorry for the last-minute change, Mae, but Jared and I are going to get a little cabin up by Lake Lanier for the weekend instead of coming home to Nantucket."

"That's a bummer!" Mae said sadly. "We're going to miss the two of you here. The fireworks show is not the same without Aunt Toni and Uncle Jared around."

"I know, I know. But I think—I think we need this."

Mae must've picked up on the shift in Toni's tone, because all she said was a soft, "Oh?"

"Yeah," Toni said, gnawing at her lip again, just like she'd been doing all day. The traffic in front of her had hardly budged since she'd gotten on the phone with Mae. Suddenly, she felt uncomfortable in the car, like she wanted to get out right this instant. Gone were the happy vibes she'd felt upon leaving the office, the certainty that this lake-house plan was the remedy for the niggling doubts she had done her best to ignore for months now. In their place, she just felt clammy and itchy and impatient.

"Is everything okay with the two of you?" Mae asked carefully.

Toni thought about unloading the blabbing stream-of-consciousness anxieties she'd kept bottled up for so long. It still wouldn't make any sense, and there was no telling if it would make her feel any better. But she felt the urge to do so nonetheless.

The problem was that Mae wouldn't understand. That wasn't her fault—it was just that she and Toni's brother, Henry, were so head-over-heels in love with each other that there wasn't even the slightest bit of room for doubts to creep in.

It would be wrong of Toni to be jealous of that. It was such a sweet thing that a love like theirs could exist in this world. Whenever she saw the two of them holding hands under the dinner table or glanced at a family picture and saw Henry's protective arm draped over Mae's shoulders, her heart softened a little bit.

But it always hardened up again right after. Because, as much as she wanted that from Jared, it wasn't forthcoming.

Yet.

Maybe things were going to change. Maybe, like a good wine, her marriage just needed some time to mature into something delicate and beautiful, like what Henry and Mae had.

The story sounded convincing enough that she decided not to answer Mae's question honestly. So, instead of opening up, she blew a stray hair back from her forehead and said with a laugh in her voice, "Oh, we're lovely. Better than ever, actually. Jared just got hired for a big project that starts the week of the holiday, though, so we couldn't find a way to make the travel work. This was the next best thing."

"Oh, well, that's fabulous then!" Mae said cheerily.

"Yeah, yeah," Toni said, still clinging to the bravado she'd mustered up. "Anyway, sorry to cut you off, but traffic is a bear right now, so I should probably focus on driving."

"Of course. Love you, Toni. Talk soon. And if we don't speak before then, have a lovely trip to the lake!"

"Love you too, Mae. Tell my oaf of a brother and your sweet little kids I said hello."

"Will do. Buh-bye."

They hung up, and Toni let the phone fall in her lap. Part of her was sad that they wouldn't be going to Nantucket. There was no place quite like her home. But after the phone call with Mae, she suddenly wasn't sure that going there would be a good idea either.

Mae loved her husband and loved her kids, and they all loved her. They had a happy home, a full home.

And that, more than anything, was what Toni was missing.

She and Jared had chatted about having children on and off through the years, though it had never led anywhere. Jared hadn't ever said it outright, but Toni got the feeling that he had no intention of raising a family. At least, no intention of raising a family *with her.*

Perhaps it wasn't fair to him to add that last part, since he'd given no indication that it was something wrong with Toni in particular that stood in the way of their having kids together. But she just had a feeling. And, like the feelings of doubt creeping into her relationship, it wouldn't go away, no matter how hard she tried to ignore it.

The lake would fix things. She looked in the rear-view mirror and said it out loud, as if to test the truth of it. "The lake will fix things."

*Say it again,* she whispered internally. *One more time, with feeling.*

"The lake will fix things."

She wanted so badly to believe it. But in the musty silence of the car, it didn't sound convincing at all.

# 2

## EIGHTEEN YEARS LATER

Toni isn't sure how she is supposed to feel.

Perhaps Mae said it best of all: *"I've never felt quite so useless."* That feels partially right. In any case, it captures something of what is happening in Toni's head and in her heart and in the pit of her stomach.

She feels adrift in a way, like a buoy out at sea cut loose from its moorings, reduced to nothing more than a metallic jellyfish at the mercy of the wind and the tides. She hasn't been able to do much of anything for days now, because as soon as she starts a chore—takes a shower, makes her bed, cooks a meal—she immediately loses all energy for it. Getting ready for the funeral yesterday morning felt like the most Herculean struggle she'd ever faced.

It has been like this since she first got the news about Henry. How could that have been only three days ago? It feels like a lifetime. A phone call from Mae, three little words—*Henry is dead*—and just like that, home is no longer the place she once thought it was.

Because what is Nantucket without Henry? Nantucket *is* Henry, and Henry is Nantucket. He's a sailor with a Southern twang, he's friends with the bartenders at every watering hole on the island, he looks good in Nantucket red. He laughs loud and shakes the neighbors' hands and can tell just by cocking an ear to the wind which of the two ferries is pulling up to the docks.

*Past tense,* Toni reminds herself. *He's gone. You have to start using the past tense.*

God, the air feels so heavy. Is it unseasonably humid, or is she right in her suspicion that the breeze itself is trying its best to pin her in place, grabbing onto her like clammy fingers, mussing her hair and prodding a thumb in her eye?

Her thoughts are jumbled and senseless. She put on a brave face at the church yesterday, of course. That goes without saying. Toni Benson has spent a lifetime putting on a brave face, through everything that happened with Jared and the inn and in between. Now does not seem like the appropriate time to stop. It just suddenly feels much, much harder to keep doing what she's always done.

But her family needs her bravery. The kids need it. Mae especially needs it. Toni and her sister-in-law—though really, she's been more like a true sister for a long time now—hugged each other at the funeral after everyone else filed out to the gravesite for the actual burial. And that hug felt like it lasted a thousand years. Hugging Mae is as close as Toni is ever going to get to actually laying hands on the sorrow of losing her brother. When she hugged Mae, she could feel in the rustle of their clothes and the tremor of their bones that they were going through the same sadness together.

That was the first moment in three days that Toni felt there might yet be a light at the end of the tunnel.

When Mae asked what Toni would do now, Toni said out loud what she'd been thinking since the moment she first received the phone call: "I can't stay here."

Nantucket is Henry. Henry is Nantucket. So if Henry is gone, then so is the island, or at least, the island as she has always known it.

She may have been born here, she may have grown up here, but she can't stay here. She needs to be somewhere else right now. As far away as possible, ideally.

She feels guilty for that. Is this running away again? She's done that before, and it worked out for her back then, but she's harbored a sneaking suspicion ever since then that she may have just gotten lucky that one time. Rolling the dice again could spell disaster.

What choice does she have, though? Staying here is wallowing.

That does it, then. No more delaying what must come next. She needs to go.

Sighing, she finishes locking the door to the Sweet Island Inn, her home of the last eighteen years. She drops the key into the envelope waiting in her other hand, seals it, then hides it behind the lavender hydrangea that sits to the left of the front entryway. Mae will know where to look.

She turns and rolls her suitcase down the walkway. There is a taxi at the end of the drive, waiting to whisk her away to the airport. Toni makes a promise to herself that she will not look back.

But the promise does not last. How could it? This is her home that is receding in the distance behind her. This is her life's work, her heart and soul. She built this from just a few rotting boards and a caved-in roof. Poured everything she had into it and watched it bloom.

So halfway down the drive, she stops and turns back.

The house looks calm and stoic. It is strange to see the lights turned off everywhere. The sight is made stranger still by the chill in the air and the bleak grayness of the dawn. The weather matches her mood, though, as if the island is mourning for her brother just as she is.

"Goodbye," she whispers to the building. "See you...well, I'll see you when I see you."

Then she turns, walks up to the taxi, and hands off her suitcase to the patiently waiting driver, who loads it into the trunk and then opens the rear door for her. "To the airport, right, ma'am?" he asks once they've both clambered in.

"Yes, please," she says softly.

As they pull onto the road, he asks, "Headed out for business or for pleasure?" He's gnawing on a toothpick and taking sips of a steaming hot coffee cup.

Toni considers the question for a second. She settles on an answer that isn't quite true, but may become true soon if things shake out the way she hopes.

"For adventure," she says.

The man chuckles good-naturedly. "Adventure is a good thing. Where's this adventure takin' ya?"

That is the million-dollar question. She told Mae yesterday that she might go on a cruise, if only because that required the bare minimum of thinking and planning from her. But when Toni went to find one, none were leaving soon enough to suit her. She wanted to be gone ASAP. It would have to be a flight, then.

But where to?

It is a big world, and without a home to tether her, Toni's thoughts went back to the image of the buoy cut loose and drifting chaotically on the currents of the ocean. Whoever pulls the strings of this life—fate or God or random chance—is in charge now. She is at the mercy of the winds.

Which is why she laughed when she pulled up the list of international flights and saw the first destination listed: *Buenos Aires, Argentina.*

She'd had a guest at the inn a year or two prior, a fashion designer from Argentina. The man was a talker, so when he cornered Toni, and she inquired politely about his homeland, he gushed for nearly an hour about the city of Buenos Aires.

"Oh, love, you have to go!" he said, clinging to her hand dramatically. "Tango and street art and culture like you have never seen it before! And the wine—oh God, my heart sings just to think of it."

Those things all sounded nice as Toni looked at the flight and tried to picture how it would feel to set foot there. But what sold her, when she googled the name of the city, was the very first link, a primer on all things Argentina for the novice traveler. *What does Buenos Aires mean when translated?* asked the heading halfway down the page.

The answer made her laugh out loud.

"Buenos Aires translates to 'City of Fair Winds.'"

That's what Toni Benson needs right now. If she is a jellyfish at the mercy of the ocean, then a fair wind is just what the doctor ordered.

So now she is on her way to the airport, taking the first steps of an adventure that has no end yet in sight.

≈

The flight goes as long flights always go, which is to say it is filled with equal parts anxiety and boredom. The mad dash through security, poking and prodding by the TSA agents, and then the stultifying tedium of sitting, sitting, sitting.

Sitting isn't such a bad thing for Toni right now, though. It reminds her of commuting back and forth to her job in Atlanta all those years ago. But instead of staring at the taillights of the car in front of her, she gets to gaze out the window and watch the clouds light up with the morning sun like pink and purple cotton candy.

Nantucket to Boston, Boston to Newark, Newark to Bogota, and then, at long last, Bogota to Buenos Aires. She shuffles through each stop like a zombie, just putting one foot in front of the other. She watches bad movies, drinks lukewarm coffee, and eats reheated lasagna when the flight attendants bring it around.

But mostly, she just does her best to sleep. It doesn't bring her any comfort, and she feels no better when she wakes up than she did when she first closed her eyes. And yet, it's better than thinking. Anything is better than thinking.

She wants so badly to be excited. And, in some deep part of her, she is. But that excitement sounds like it's coming from far away, as if she has been tossed down a well, and it is hollering to her from the top, way above her. She does her best to keep her focus on that, but it's so very hard when that feels distant and her grief feels so up close and personal.

The tedium of flying chips away at her ability to focus little by little, so that by the time she finally lands in Buenos Aires, she can barely think straight. She follows the passengers off the plane and down the endless fluorescent hallways. It feels like they're stuck in a labyrinth as they take turn after turn after turn. She's starting to wonder if maybe this is more of a nightmare than an adventure. That wouldn't be the worst thing. It implies the possibility of waking up and having her brother still be alive.

But eventually, they're spat out by the hallways into the lobby with the baggage carousels.

Toni is craving a glass of wine and twelve hours of dreamless sleep. She's got a car service arranged already, so all she needs to do is find her bag and go straight to her hotel.

The problem is, her bag is not here.

She stands impatiently at the back of the herd of people crowding towards the conveyor belt. One by one, they find their things and slip out to join the throng of traffic coursing past the front of the airport.

Blue bags, green bags, huge bags with hideous checkered houndstooth fabric.

But no black bag with a red ribbon tied around the handle.

Until, at long last, she finally sees it spewed out through the hanging rubber flaps. She offers up a quick hallelujah and starts to make her way through the remaining crowd.

"Excuse me. Pardon me. Sorry, I just need to…"

She's at that level of tired where even the glare of a stranger feels like a burden she can't possibly bear, so she keeps her head down and keeps moving forward.

She's about to reach the edge of the belt and grab her bag. But when she looks up, she sees that it's gone. Someone else has taken it already.

She whirls around and scans the airport lobby in bewilderment. It's a herd of people, most as tired and irritable as she is. They're wheeling suitcases of all colors and shapes. But she doesn't see hers. Until…

Bingo. She spots the thief.

Even in her deep state of exhaustion, she can tell that the man currently wheeling her bag towards the exit is handsome. He's tall and broad, with salt-and-pepper hair and a smooth olive complexion. The hand gripping the suitcase handle looks strong and capable, and in profile, she sees a razor-sharp jaw, covered in a day or two's worth of artfully curated stubble. The suit he's wearing screams that he's a businessman of some sort—navy, neatly pressed even after a long flight, with polished brown leather shoes to match.

"Excuse me!" she calls ahead. But the man takes one step for every two of hers and still manages to widen the distance between them.

She yells it again, "Excuse me!" And still, he does not turn around.

Growling, she lowers her head like a sprinter and charges forward. A few other travelers leap back in alarm, though she pays them no mind.

Finally, she catches up to the handsome businessman, seizes his forearm, and yanks him back towards her.

He turns around, and she sees that she was absolutely right about his good looks. He's got thick, dark, expressive eyebrows that are currently arrowed downwards in irritation.

"*Sí?*" he snaps. "*Qué te pasa?*"

She doesn't appreciate his tone at all. The fact that she didn't understand what he said doesn't help matters. However, embarrassingly, Toni is a little out of breath from her mad dash to catch up with this man and stop him from running away with her luggage. So it takes her a second to get her wind back, swallow, brush the flyaways out of her face, and announce, "You have my bag."

She points down at the suitcase to illustrate what she's saying. To her further annoyance, though, the man shakes his head dismissively, not even bothering to look where she's pointing.

"No," he replies curtly in a faint Latin accent, "I do not."

He starts to turn around again as if that settles it. In alarm, Toni grabs his forearm a second time.

"Yes," she repeats with a stubborn set to her mouth, "you do. Black bag with a red ribbon. That's mine."

The man clicks his tongue, a habit that has always driven Toni up the wall. Jared used to do that.

"*Qué quilombo, chabona,*" he mutters under his breath. Toni doesn't know any Spanish that wasn't taught in Señorita Smith's ninth-grade class at Nantucket High, but it doesn't take a rocket scientist to know that the man didn't say anything nice. "Madam," he continues, "*my* bag is black with a red ribbon. This is mine. Thank you."

He looks like he's about to turn away for a second time, but before he can, Toni bends down and grabs the luggage tag tied next to the red ribbon on the handle. "Look!" she exclaims. "Toni Benson. That's me. Can I have my bag now, please?"

The businessman frowns. He leans over next to her and pulls the tag rudely out of her hands. Examining it himself, he clicks his tongue again, then straightens up.

"Oh," is all he says.

Toni is inches away from picking a fight with this guy. A mix-up, sure, no problem. But he doesn't have to be such a pig about it, does he? She's had a long flight. A long week. Her brother is dead, her home is forever tarnished.

She tries to remind herself that maybe this guy is going through something similar, to give him the benefit of the doubt. After all, there's that thing they say about strangers—"You never know what battles someone else is fighting." It's not out of the question that he needs her patience just as much as she needs his.

But the condescending set to his mouth says otherwise.

The man spends one long moment looking at her. Despite the condescending twist of his mouth, he really is quite lovely to look at. Those gray eyes are piercing, almost to the point of being harsh. She feels seen in a strange way. It's not nice, but it's not necessarily unpleasant, either. It's as if the whole rest of the airport disappeared in this man's vision and she is all he can see.

Then he blinks and nods and is gone without saying another word.

Toni shakes her head. Sorrow and sleep deprivation are dealing her a nasty double whammy. Forget the glass of wine she'd been envisioning throughout the entire flight—she just wants to get straight to bed.

But by the time she finds her driver, gets to her hotel, checks in, and makes it to her room, the insatiable craving for sleep is gone. It's late at this point, nearly midnight, and she's been traveling for just under thirty-six hours. Surely her body and brain could use the rest?

And yet, sleep will not come.

She lies in the soft queen bed, staring at the whirling blades of the ceiling fan overhead. Her mind, far from being quiet, is racing.

She misses her brother. Henry would've known what to do with that man at the airport. He would've probably ended up befriending the guy and inviting him over for a whiskey at the hotel bar.

She misses her home. The thought of the Sweet Island Inn sitting vacant and dormant is weirdly unsettling. For eighteen years, it's been a beehive of comings and goings. She's had guests come and never leave. She's watched them grow; she herself has grown. Now, though, it is just a building. Some essential part of it feels snuffed out.

Most confusingly, she misses the family she never had. On the flight from Newark to Bogota, there had been a family seated on the other side of the aisle. A handsome redhead man and his petite brunette wife. She had a baby on her lap, while her husband was kept busy playing UNO with their polite little boy, whose legs were too short to reach the floor, so they swung back and forth beneath his seat. Toni had watched them for a while. It made her heart ache to see something so simple—a mother holding a baby, a father teaching his son how not to tip his cards. How many moments are there like that in the life of a family? Thousands—millions, even. This foursome would probably never remember this flight. But it is stamped in Toni's memory indelibly, all the more special because there was nothing special about it to them.

She wonders what it would have been like if everything had gone right. Would she have been the one holding a sleeping baby while her husband played games with their son? Perhaps.

What else would be different? There would be no Sweet Island Inn, of course. She might live in Atlanta, not Nantucket.

And maybe her brother would still be alive.

That's a preposterous thought, and she does her best to dismiss it out of hand. But it lingers anyway, like a stain she cannot scrub away. She tells the empty hotel room, "That's ridiculous," and for a second, that does the trick.

But when her voice fades away, the thought crops back up again, as stubborn as Henry himself.

Toni sits upright with an irritated growl. Forget sleeping. Maybe that glass of wine is what she needs after all.

Throwing off the comforter, she goes over to her suitcase and quickly pulls on a pair of jeans, a white cotton top, and slips her feet into her sandals. She tucks her room key into her back pocket and makes her way downstairs to the hotel bar.

It's mostly empty when she gets there. There is only one other drinker, a chic-looking woman with long, dark hair, contemplating a martini set on the marble bar top in front of her. Behind the bar, a man in suspenders and a black felt driver's cap browses his phone idly.

Toni slides into one of the big, high-backed black leather chairs and folds her hands in her lap. The bartender glances up. "What can I get you?" he asks in a lightly accented voice. He doesn't even bother going with Spanish first. She must really look out of place.

"Uh, Malbec, please," she says. It's what that guest at the inn years ago had recommended so highly.

He nods and turns to pour her the glass of wine. When it is full, he sets it down on a cocktail napkin in front of her and shifts his attention back to his cell phone.

Toni takes a tentative sip of the drink. "Oh my!" she gasps out loud when she does—the fashion designer from Argentina wasn't lying about the country's famous wine. It is dry, full-bodied, and so rich, with vanilla and dark chocolate swirling between layers of juicy oakyness.

She looks around, sees the woman at the other end of the bar looking at her, and turns her eyes downward in embarrassment. The bartender doesn't seem to notice anything that's happening beyond his cell-phone screen.

"It is good, no?"

Toni glances back up. It was the woman at the bar with her who spoke. If Toni's not mistaken, she had a French accent. No speakers anywhere else in the world have quite that same manner of speaking in a single string of syllables, all flowing, lilting highs-and-lows.

"It's amazing, honestly," Toni said. "I was ready to be disappointed."

The woman laughs. It sounds like a wind chime. She's so effortlessly classy, Toni thinks to herself, the kind of woman who can be drinking in a hotel bar at midnight by herself and look like she's precisely where she's meant to be. For her part, Toni feels like a wreck. Underdressed, exhausted, and somehow tight, as if there are wires of tension under her skin and behind her eyes that are being pulled taut.

"They do know their wine, these *porteños.*"

Toni nods. "It would certainly seem so. I'm sorry, what was the last thing you said?"

"*Porteños,*" the woman repeats, enunciating carefully. "It means 'people of the port." She waves a hand around as if to indicate the whole city. "People who live here in Buenos Aires, you know?"

"Ah," Toni says. "Got it." She feels dumb and American already, and so wildly far from home that she wonders why on earth she ever thought this was a good idea.

The woman smiles, though, and that makes her feel a little better. "Where are you from?" she asks.

"America," Toni says after taking another sip of the wine. She can already feel it working its way through her system, sandpapering off some of the edge that has been rubbing her the wrong way ever since the encounter with the businessman at the airport. "The Northeast. A little island up there called Nantucket."

"Nantucket, yes," the woman muses. "I have heard of this. It is beautiful, is it not?"

"Very."

"You are a long way from home, though."

Toni laughs bitterly. "It certainly feels that way," she says in a near-whisper.

"And what brings you to the land of tango?"

"Oh, you know..." Toni says, gesturing vaguely. She feels a sudden lump in her throat. It hadn't yet occurred to her that people would ask that question. She knows that's stupid—it's one of the first things she asks all the guests of the inn—and yet it just never came up in her planning. Now, with the question thrust upon her, the thought of answering honestly, of explaining that her brother has died and she badly needed to run from her grief, feels ridiculous.

"...Just taking a little 'me time,'" she finishes lamely. She crosses her fingers next to her thigh and hopes the woman does not press further.

Thankfully, she doesn't, though it's hard to say whether it's because she doesn't care or because she notices Toni's sudden reluctance.

"We could all do with more of that," the woman says with another flash of a friendly grin. "I am Camille, by the way." She slides out of her seat gracefully and comes over to Toni. Toni is prepared to shake her hand, but the woman instead leans forward and kisses her once on each cheek. Mae loves to do that, too, and in this small, simple gesture, Toni feels a sudden rush of affection for this kind stranger.

"I'm Toni," she answers quietly. Part of her is concerned that she is about to fall weeping into Camille's arms. She's feeling very unstable all of a sudden.

"It is a pleasure to meet you, Toni," says Camille. "I am going now. Will you be here for some time?"

"Until I finish the wine, I guess."

Camille laughs again. Like everything else she does, it is elegant.

"I meant in the city, Toni."

"Oh," Toni says, blushing. "Yes. For some time."

"Good. Perhaps we will share a drink together again, then. *Adieu.*"

And then, she is gone, whisking away to the elevator bank and disappearing within.

Toni watches her go, then finishes her wine quietly. When it's done, she charges her tab to the room before going back upstairs.

In the dark silence of her hotel room, she undresses and slips once more under the comforter. This time, sleep rushes on her quickly. Her last thought before she falls gratefully into its arms—and she knows it's a silly thought for a woman approaching sixty years of age—is that maybe this trip won't be so bad.

After all, she made a friend today.

# 3

ATLANTA, GEORGIA—JULY 1, 2000

Toni glanced nervously at the package strapped into her passenger seat. Maybe this was going too far.

But who could blame her? Over the last two weeks since she'd officially booked the lake-house cabin, Toni's excitement had turned into anxiety and her anxiety into excitement, over and over again like a snake eating its own tail until she couldn't tell where one stopped and the other began.

Which was not to say that going to the bakery and having them design a cake in the shape of a log cabin was necessarily justified. But if she didn't do *something* to channel her nervous, bubbling energy, Toni felt like she might just explode.

So that is how the log cabin ice-cream cake came to be sitting on the front passenger seat of her car—seat-belted in for safety, of course, Atlanta traffic being what it was—as she headed home on her lunch break to surprise Jared with all that she had in store for him: the cake, their plans, her love.

"C'mon, c'mon," she urged the drivers in front of her. Everyone in town seemed to be moving slow as molasses today. It was like they were purposefully trying to delay her and make her even crazier than she already felt.

Little by little, she inched closer towards home. She slid from the highway onto the frontage road, from the frontage road onto her street, from her street into her driveway.

Jared's car was parked out front. He often worked from home or from a nearby coffee shop if he wasn't out at a client meeting. He'd probably be a little irritable at her unexpectedly interrupting him, but oh well, the grouch would just have to get over it.

Toni was smiling to herself, humming a little as she got out of the car and scurried around to the other side to carefully extract the cake. She strode up to the door and wriggled it open with her free hand. It swung inward on quiet hinges, and she slipped into the house.

With any luck, Jared had his headphones on and wouldn't have heard her coming inside. There was a little voice in her head that kept repeating what he'd said that night outside the restaurant on his thirty-fifth birthday— *"I don't like surprises"*—but she dismissed it.

This wasn't just any old surprise. In her head, it was everything. She'd show him that, and when he saw it through Toni's eyes, Jared would get it. He could be so sharp like that sometimes. She'd never been the best at phrasing her thoughts, but Jared knew her inside and out. If she fumbled over how to express something, he could just get it in an instant and say it exactly how it ought to be said. It was nice to be understood like that.

She pushed the door closed behind her with a hip, wincing as the latch clicked into place. Her heart was beating fast, she noticed, so she closed her eyes and took a deep breath.

It felt—stupidly, she knew, and yet she couldn't deny that the feeling in her chest—like she was holding her marriage in her hands, in the form of this silly little cake. All she had to do was go down the hallway to Jared's home office and show it to him, and the rest of their lives would cruise easily along, no more friction, no more problems.

She slipped off her shoes so she could sneak up more quietly and stifled a nervous giggle. Then, moving toe to heel with each stride, so she didn't cause any of the wooden floorboards to groan, she rounded the corner and turned down the hallway.

The sides of the hallway were lined with pictures of them from the last twelve years, in roughly chronological order. Toni walked slowly, looking at each of them and smiling as she passed.

There was one from shortly after their first date when they'd gone to Six Flags, the two of them both screaming and throwing their hands in the air as a roller coaster took their breath away.

There was one from their first Christmas together. They'd gone to Nantucket and celebrated with Henry and Mae and Toni's nieces and nephews. It was snowing in the picture, and they were all bundled up like little felt bowling balls. Jared's nose was bright red. Toni had teased him by calling him Rudolph all week long.

There was the snapshot that Jared's buddy Carlos had taken of the moment he proposed to her. They'd gone to a botanical garden, and Jared had dropped to a knee in the middle of a cloud of beautiful monarch butterflies and revealed a ring in a velvet box. Toni only remembered bits and pieces of the speech he gave, but who cared about details like that?

Then, the wedding and the honeymoon, a cluster from each of them. She'd always particularly loved the black-and-white shot of the two of them walking out through the doors of the church, holding hands, with grains of rice forever suspended in the air above them. She looked so happy in that one.

The last picture before she reached the doorway to Jared's office was of just Toni. Jared had snapped it during a summer trip back home to Nantucket. She was wheeling her bike down the beach towards the water and gazing calmly into the distance. She was wearing a simple white dress with her hair loose and long and sashaying idly in the soft breeze. In the distance, a squat white lighthouse kept an eye on the horizon.

She'd always loved that one. It was beachy and romantic. But as she looked at it now, she didn't get the same warm fuzzies she usually did whenever it happened to catch her eye. Normally, she would've said that she looked at peace, perfectly content, even though the picture didn't show much of her face.

But now, she saw it from a different angle. The Toni in the photograph wasn't some Zen woman suffused with joy and contentment.

She was lonely, looking out into the distance as if hoping that someone or something was going to come hurtling towards her bearing a sense of purpose on a silver platter.

She barely had time to register those disquieting thoughts, much less to process them, before two things occurred to her at once.

The first thing was that, when she'd slipped off her shoes by the door, there had been an unfamiliar pair of shoes lined up against the wall there. Why she was just now realizing that, she couldn't say, but it hit her like a blunt object. A pair of black women's pumps, with one buckle busted. They did not belong to Toni, or to this house.

The second thing was that there was a noise coming from the office. Two noises in one, actually. Voices. Breathing. Heavy panting, to be precise.

So when Toni pushed open the door of the office and caught a glimpse of her husband cheating on her, it wouldn't be quite right to say that she was surprised. Because she had known at once what those noises had indicated. And she knew what it meant for her, too: that her life as she had known it was over, as suddenly and irrevocably as the drop of a guillotine cleaving her past from her future.

She fainted. The cake in her hands fell and hit the floor. Icing flew everywhere. Her last sight, before everything went completely black, was a smear of blue cream on the doorframe. It dripped down, down, down.

It hit the floor. Only then did she fully give in to the rush of darkness.

$$\sim$$

Eleven years and fifty-one weeks before she dropped the cake and passed out in the hallway of the home she shared with the man who was cheating on her, Toni Benson had been walking down a dark and quiet street with that very same man.

It was close to midnight, and they'd been drinking for hours at a quiet little bar in Virginia Highlands, so she had a pleasant buzz coursing through her head, making the world seem pastel and welcoming.

As far as first dates went, it had gone extremely well in that he seemed charming, smart, and handsome, the last of which she already knew. But it was nonetheless nice to be seated across from him again and confirm that she hadn't just made that fact up in her mind in the couple of weeks since they'd first met at her office.

Jared stopped and playfully grabbed her hand as they passed under an old-timey gas lamp outside the door of another quiet bar. "I can't in good conscience let the night end here, can I?" he mused. He pulled her close to him so that they could both feel the heat of the lamp wafting over them. He smelled nice—a woodsy cologne layered on top of a clean, masculine soap scent—and when she rested a hand on his chest without thinking much of it, she noticed that it was stronger and more muscled than she might've otherwise suspected, what with him being a computer programmer and all.

"I don't know," Toni replied, biting her lip to hide a teasing smile. "Can you?"

"It just wouldn't be right," Jared said solemnly before cracking a grin of his own. He had a cleft chin, what Toni's mom would've called a Superman chin, and it was absurd how good-looking she found that silly little feature.

As tipsy as she was, she was only just now beginning to suspect that they were hurtling towards their first kiss. It was a little faster than she might've planned if she'd had time to stop and think about it, but they'd been hanging out for hours now; they'd shared cocktails and good conversation. Given that he had only been in her office for maybe an hour or two, he was awfully good at doing impersonations of all the people she worked with. Sabrina's cackle and Marlon's baritone boom and the way Damon, the lead partner who saw himself as the firm's alpha male, liked to hold his arms perfectly still and flexed at his sides as he walked down the hallway, as if to show everyone how strong he was. Jared did each of them in turn, and Toni laughed louder and louder with each one, until the two of them subsided into the kind of tense but not uncomfortable silently-staring-into-each-other's-eyes that invariably happens in the final third of a good first date.

The back of her mind was swimming with the sorts of silly images that crop up in a moment like that: white picket fences and church bells ringing and the idle pondering of whether their kids would have Jared's copper curls or blonde hair like hers. She put those aside and focused instead on that country-boy smile.

As they stood under the gas lamp and the occasional passerby studiously avoided eye contact while they strode down the sidewalk, it felt like they'd stepped into a candlelit bubble and found that moment. Jared looked at Toni, and Toni looked at Jared, and for a second, the rest of the world ceased to exist.

He kissed her, softly and chastely, and then let her go. Toni's hand never left his chest. She could feel his heart beating.

*Ba-boom, ba-boom.*

*Ba-boom, ba-boom.*

$$\sim$$

"Toni."

Toni's eyes fluttered open. Jared's face was right up in hers. She saw him leap backward as if shocked to see her awake. For a moment, he looked terrified, like a little kid called to the principal's office. Then a mask of hardened ice settled over his features, and the look of fear was gone.

"Are you okay?" he asked. There wasn't an ounce of softness in his voice.

"I...I think so." Toni sat up. She was laid out on the couch in the living room. Jared had put on a pair of raggedy jeans and an old white T-shirt, which was two items of clothing more than he'd been wearing when she opened the door of his office. "How long have I been out?"

"Just a couple of minutes. I brought you here. You hit your head pretty hard on the wall." He stood on the far side of the room, leaning against the doorframe that led to the kitchen, arms folded across his chest.

Toni reached up and felt her forehead. She winced when her fingers brushed across a knot at her right temple. That was going to turn into a gnarly bruise.

She straightened up a little more, groaning as she did. Her mouth tasted like blood, although her finger came away clean when she poked the inside of her cheek.

She didn't want to look at Jared, so she looked around. Strange how somewhere that was once home can become something other than that in a single instant. The pictures on the walls, the pillows on the couch—she'd chosen all of them, and yet they suddenly felt foreign, staged, as if she'd never seen them before.

She did her best to avoid it, but eventually, the magnetic pull of the hallway was too strong, so she looked down there, too. She saw blue cake frosting smeared on the wall. There was a rectangle of light cast onto the floor, emanating from Jared's office, and as she watched, she saw a shadow pass across it and then retreat again.

Toni's jaw clenched. "Who is she?" She stared down at her hands as she spoke. They were trembling.

"No one," Jared said. At the very uppermost edge of Toni's vision, she saw him shake his head. That only made her madder.

"Who is she?" she repeated hollowly.

Jared sighed. "I don't want to do this right now."

That made her look up at him. "Do you think I want to do this right now, Jared?"

He said nothing, did nothing, just looked back at her with an unreadable blankness in his eyes.

"Heather," he answered finally.

All Toni could say was, "Ah."

That made sense. Heather was his "secretary," as Jared had explained it, though why a one-man software operation would need a secretary had never made sense to Toni. Particularly not a twenty-seven-year-old secretary with a loud giggle and a propensity for high heels. The girl had been respectful to Toni on the few occasions when they'd met, which went some ways towards assuaging the stupid doubts that inevitably crop up in the mind of a woman in her late thirties whose husband has just hired a curvy young thing to work for him. Toni wasn't a jealous woman or an insecure one; so as long as the girl could look her in the eye and converse politely, she'd never paid her much attention.

That, it turned out, was a stupid error.

"How long?" Toni asked quietly.

Jared sighed again, like this was all some big drag on his mood. "I said I don't want to do this right now, Toni."

Toni bit her lip. Part of her wanted to do this, to drag all the answers out into the light and rage at them. But part of her was suddenly tired. She felt like she could crawl into her bed and sleep for days, weeks, months, years.

Although she realized with a sudden pang, it wasn't her bed anymore. And who knows how long it had been like that? How many times had Heather slept there, curled up against her husband's side, feeling the heartbeat that Toni had felt under that gas lamp almost a dozen years ago? Toni was immediately overwhelmed by the haunting, nauseating feeling one gets after a house break-in. Someone had been in her home, treading in her footsteps, touching her things, all without her knowledge or consent. She grabbed the pillow next to her and hugged it tightly like it could anchor her surging anxieties and stop them from drowning her.

"I'm sorry it happened like this," Jared said with sudden sharpness, "but it's best that it happened sooner rather than later, I guess."

"So that's it then."

"Yes."

"Yes?"

"Yes, that's it."

What an answer! It was both wildly inadequate, and yet somehow, it was also all that needed to be said. She didn't want to hear anything else he had to say. Not the how or the why or the when.

All she wanted was to be out of this stranger's house. It belonged to an old version of her, or to her soon-to-be ex-husband and his new woman, and she no longer wanted to be under this roof because if she stayed here much longer then it would shrink around her and suffocate her. She wanted out.

So she stood up and walked over to the entryway. She slipped on her shoes, grabbed her keys, and walked out the door. She half expected Jared to say something—"I'm sorry" or "I'll let you know when you can come get your stuff" or even just a limp "Goodbye, Toni." But he said none of those things. She couldn't decide if she appreciated his silence or if she despised him for it.

The summer air greeted Toni on the front stoop like an unwelcome dog licking her face. She went to her car, got in, and sat there in silence with the keys lying in her hand. A lot had happened in the last fifteen minutes. In fact, the inside of the car was still cool from the air conditioning.

She closed her eyes and breathed. Two truths were staring her in the face: either her marriage was a lie all along, or it was a good thing that she would never have again. Toni wasn't sure which option was worse.

# 4

BUENOS AIRES, ARGENTINA—MAY 5, 2018

"Toni, come out and show me!" Camille calls in her smooth trill.

"Absolutely not," Toni responds at once. She is standing in the dressing room of the little boutique in the Palermo neighborhood, where Camille has dragged her, looking in the mirror and seeing what feels like a completely different woman gazing back out at her.

It isn't just the dress she's trying on that is throwing her for a loop, though that is certainly where a lot of the questions in her head begin and end. After all, Toni Benson is a born-and-raised Nantucket native. She has never stepped so much as a single toe in what Camille taught her is called a *milonga*, the Argentine term for a party where the national dance, tango, is performed.

"Like a sock hop?" Toni had asked and then immediately regretted asking.

Luckily, by the way she wrinkled her nose in confusion, it was clear that Camille didn't know what a sock hop was, so Toni was spared the embarrassment of dating herself so badly.

"A *milonga* is a celebration, a festival, a ritual," Camille eventually explained in that poetic, indirect way of hers. "There are rules that must be followed, but we will get there in time. The first order of business is your attire."

Which is what brought them to this boutique, a cute shop with flowers in the windows and an exquisitely made-up saleswoman smoking a cigarette out front. When Camille explained to the woman in a flurry of Spanish what they were looking for, the woman stubbed out her cigarette, gave Toni a once-over with a discerning eye, and led her inside by the crook of her elbow. Toni found herself poked, prodded, measured with a length of tape, and deposited—not rudely, but firmly—into a dressing room.

Then, one after the other, came the dresses.

They were dresses like Toni had never seen before. Shocking in color, daring in cut, the kind of thing she would never in a million years choose for herself. After all, she was a fifty-seven-year-old divorcée with a bad left knee, not a young Latina heartbreaker with swiveling hips and hardly a care in the world!

But Camille and the saleswoman have thus far merely shushed right over her protests and continued to throw dresses over the door. Feeling cornered and overwhelmed, Toni has decided it is easier to do things their way for the time being.

For a Frenchwoman, Camille knows an awful lot about Argentine culture. The way she tells her story, she came here years ago and fell in love with the country and its people. After a divorce, she made one more trip from her homeland to Buenos Aires and simply stayed put. Her accent has remained French, but everything else about her swoons with that distinctly *porteño* mélange of European classiness and South American fire.

Toni is glad that the two of them met by chance on her first night here. It has been one month since she landed in Argentina, and Camille has been a near-constant companion since the day of her arrival. They've shared coffee, walks through the park, and trips to the national museum to look at the beautiful art kept on display there. Camille has also been urging Toni to join her on a wild night out. Thus far, Toni has begged out of it every time.

The truth of the matter is that Toni's heart is still sore. She cries herself to sleep as often as not. The loss of a brother is an unfathomable thing under the best of circumstances, and she is a long, long way from finding a bottom on which to plant her feet.

But, time being what it is, she is finding it harder and harder to refuse Camille's pleas. "It will be fun!" she cries whenever they discuss the prospect. "No one is asking you to do anything but dance, *chica*."

"I can't dance to save my life," Toni has pointed out on more than one occasion.

And each time, Camille offers up the same proverb: "It's like the Japanese say, Toni—'We're fools whether we dance or not, so we might as well dance.'" And each time, she nods and smiles enigmatically, as if that settles things.

This little power struggle over the issue of the dresses is merely an extension of the bickering they've been having for a month. That Toni is here, trying them on, is surely evidence that she is fighting a losing battle.

But there is something about the garment she is wearing that almost makes her want to lose.

This most recent dress—the eleventh or twelfth one Toni has tried on —is doing something in her reflection that Toni can't quite wrap her head around. It is the crisp red of a fresh-bloomed rose, with thin straps over her shoulders and a graceful knot tied in the center of her chest. The fabric hugs her torso and her hips as it descends into a scalloped hem just above her knees.

She looks like how she has not felt in a very long time: powerful, confident, capable. She looks like a woman who knows how to tango and what wine to order with her dinner and how to navigate the grief brought on by tragedy. And even if she doesn't feel those things in her heart of hearts, the dress tells her that perhaps she is a bit closer to feeling them than she was before she put it on.

"These, too!" Camille chirps. She slides a pair of black stilettos under the door.

Sighing, Toni dutifully slips them on, buckling the straps around her ankles. When she stands up again, she cannot help but smile, even if she feels like she is far over her head.

She swallows, takes a deep breath, and opens the dressing room door.

"*Bellissima!*" the saleswoman says with the air of a craftsman who has measured and cut perfectly.

Camille just smiles.

"Are you sure it's not too much?" Toni says. She feels guilty for saying it because it's obvious to everyone in the room that it's perfect. It just feels like the sort of thing she is supposed to say in this scenario.

Camille touches her softly on the shoulder. "It is right," she says softly.

Toni steps up to the platform in front of the three-sided mirror and does a nervous twirl. The dress flares out slightly as she pirouettes, and the heels make a soft, rhythmic tapping noise beneath her.

"Okay," she says finally. She turns back to look at Camille and smiles. "Let's go dancing."

～

After a nap, a shower, dinner at a small café with Camille where they chitchat about anything except for the night's upcoming festivities, and then a return to Toni's hotel to finish getting ready for the *milonga*, Toni finds herself seated in a chair at the outer rim of a large, empty ballroom. The wooden floor gleams under the warm lights overhead. All around her, people are buzzing in. Some bear broad smiles and big laughter, but many of them look just as nervous as she does.

"*Cálmate,*" Camille tells Toni, resting a hand on her knee. "It is only dancing."

"Sorry," Toni apologizes. She hadn't realized that she was bouncing her knee quite so ferociously. It's a nervous habit that she hasn't been able to shed in nearly sixty years of living, no matter how hard she tries.

"What frightens you?"

"Everything," Toni answers immediately. She blushes. It is hot beneath the lights, though they dim a bit almost as soon as she thinks that.

"But there is nothing to fear, no?"

"Tripping, falling, stumbling, face planting, elbowing someone in the face...The list is endless, really."

"Ah, ah," Camille tuts like a schoolteacher. "Happy thinking only, Toni."

"Yeah, yeah, yeah," Toni mutters back. She's shooting nervous glances around the room, trying to reassure herself that she cannot possibly be the worst dancer or the most nervous person in the room.

But, rather than finding reassurance, what she finds instead is a shock sighting straight out of left field.

The door to the room sweeps open, and in walks someone she was sure she would never see again: the businessman from the airport.

She's almost positive it is the same man, even though his hair is a touch longer and more unruly. He has paused in a patch of shadow, so she can't see half of his face clearly. But the image of that broad, strong hand holding onto the handle of her baggage is seared permanently into her memory.

As she watches, he straightens the cuffs of the white shirt he is wearing beneath his pale gray suit. It's the same hands; she's sure of it.

"Are you all right?" Camille asks. "You look like you've seen a ghost." She follows Toni's line of sight, sees who she is looking at, and frowns. "Do you know that man?"

"Not really," Toni says, shaking her head dismissively. "Just a random...never mind. Don't worry about it. It's not important."

Thankfully, a bell chimes just then, and a woman with the same stern, searingly beautiful style as the saleswoman at the tango dress boutique steps into the center of the circle. Her dark hair is pulled back in a severe bun, and her lipstick is a burgundy that looks gorgeous against her pale skin.

"*Bienvenidos* and welcome," she begins in a rapid lilt. "I am your instructor for the evening." Her words all flow together, joined like steps in a dance. Toni finds herself sitting up in her chair a little straighter, unconsciously prodded upwards by the woman's perfect posture.

The instructor goes through a spiel about the evening's proceedings that Toni only half listens to. Instead, she finds herself glancing again and again at the man from the airport. He is seated on the far side of the room, still in the shadows, leaning back in his chair with his ankle crossed over his knee. He looks arrogant, rigid, and composed. He does not look back towards her, not even once.

It is hard to pay attention over the next hour as the woman tutors all the newcomers, like Toni, who need instruction on the basics of the tango before the evening's actual festivities begin. Even as Toni is paired with a mild-mannered Brit who steps on her feet more than once with a thud and a "Sorry," she looks out of the corner of her eye periodically to see if the businessman has budged. He hasn't, not even once. He keeps his hands folded in his lap and watches the beginners fumble around.

She's not sure why, but his presence here is irritating her. And the way he's just *sitting* there, as if he owns the place, as if all this amateurish ineptness amuses him—it simply isn't right. There's a part of her that yearns to give him a piece of her mind.

The intensity of the emotion surprises her. Throughout her entire life, she has never been one for melodramatic outbursts. "You Bensons are an even-keeled clan," Mae has mentioned with a chuckle more than once while eyeing Toni and Henry. "It takes a great deal to get a rise out of you."

Toni feels like that is a fair characterization. Even all those years ago, when her marriage went supernova in a single instant, Toni didn't blow her stack. So why should this stranger be coaxing such a rise out of her? She's not sure. All she knows is that she doesn't like him. But also, she doesn't like that she doesn't like him.

The beginners trade partners, and Toni finds herself with a stocky, bearded Swede who has a little more grace to his steps than the Brit did. For her own part, Toni is getting more comfortable with the rhythm of it, the closeness of it, the pursuit and follow between dancing partners. It's nothing she would've ever dreamed of on her own, but to her great surprise, she's finding that it speaks to a part of her. She might even say that she's enjoying it, truth be told.

Camille has gone back and forth between checking her cell phone and giving Toni encouraging smiles from the sidelines. As she and the Swede stride past, Camille grins once again.

At the end of the song, the instructor calls everyone together into the middle of the dance floor and explains the rules rapid-fire in multiple languages so that all of the attendees can understand. Toni's head is spinning by the time she's finished, but she's fairly certain that she has the gist of it.

Basically, a male partner catches the eyes of a female dancer from a distance and inclines his head as an invitation to join him. If she accepts, she nods back, and they dance together for the length of a *tanda,* a three- or four-song section of music. Dancers follow the *ronda,* the pattern of movement on the floor like the flow of a river. There is no talking during the *tandas.*

Those are all of the rules, or at least Toni hopes so because those are the only ones she understood. With a firm nod, the instructor says the evening will begin shortly and dismisses them all to the chairs until then.

Toni sinks gratefully into a wooden chair next to Camille. "I am exhausted already," she complains good-naturedly.

"Pah! Nonsense. You have a lovely stride," Camille says with a friendly pat on the thigh.

"Thanks," murmurs Toni. She glances around. The room has filled up slowly over the last hour, with more and more folks eager to tango. Frowning, she searches the faces, but it looks as though the businessman is gone. *Well, good riddance,* she thinks to herself. His presence had been casting an ugly pallor over the evening anyway. It's better that he is gone.

A bell chimes out softly just then. It feels like the air in the room immediately tightens. Everyone stands up at once, Toni a half beat behind the rest of the folks in the room. "Come," Camille says, offering her hand. Toni grabs it and looks around as a sort of frenzied shuffle begins. It's the kind of moment where everyone is panicking but trying not to look like it. Or perhaps that's just Toni projecting.

She goes through the rules again in her head. Eye contact, *tandas,* follow the *ronda.* Three forward steps, a side step, a drag step... It's all blurring together in her head.

She pictures Henry laughing at her.

She pictures Jared dancing with Heather.

She pictures everyone she's ever known, kicked back in seats just like that businessman from the airport was, looking on and laughing.

Then she takes a deep breath and whisks that all aside. It's just dancing, right? No need to get all crazy about it.

As her eyes rake across the crowd, a man catches Toni's eyes. He has dark brown hair, neatly parted, and a short-cropped brown beard to match. He's wearing dark denim jeans with nice leather shoes, and the sleeves of his white button-down are rolled up to the elbow. He nods pleasantly and offers up a half smile. Toni hesitates, bites her lip, and then returns his look with a short nod.

As he strides through the throng of people percolating on the dance floor, the music begins, pouring through the speakers set high in each of the room's corners. Toni's heartbeat is throbbing in her chest. Camille squeezes her hand once, gives her a reassuring smile, and then slides away into the arms of a dark-haired man with a hairy barrel chest. She looks so effortless, like a drop of water slipping into the ocean, exactly where she belongs. Toni is jealous, but she reminds herself that no one is good at these things on their first go-around.

The man who nodded to her is waiting at the edge of the dance floor now, a few steps away. With one last anxious swallow, Toni steps towards him.

"My name is Mateo," he says.

"Toni," she mumbles, just barely audible.

He arches an eyebrow, but he must see how nervous she is because rather than asking her to repeat herself, he gives a short bow and extends his hands towards her.

She takes them, trying all the while to quell her shaking. Then they are chest to chest, and the music is at full volume, and the *tanda* has begun.

Toni spends the entirety of the first song watching her feet and mumbling the steps of the basic pattern in her head. Step-step-step, side step, drag step. Again, again, as they cruise around the edge of the circular dance floor like a record on a turntable.

By the time the first song ends and the second begins, she's feeling a bit less nervous, enough to look up at the man and grin sheepishly. "You are doing well," he murmurs.

He's a good enough dancer, though she can tell that he is doing some of the same conscious self-instruction that she is. Together, they are managing to hash it out, though. They meld into the rest of the dancers—some better than them, some much worse—without making fools of themselves, for which Toni is extraordinarily grateful.

When the *tanda* ends, Mateo returns Toni to the seat where she was before. He smiles and does that stiff, quirky half bow again before dropping back into the melee of people.

Camille arrives and collapses into the chair at Toni's left. "So?" she exclaims. "How was it?" She is glowing with life. Her side-bangs wick away droplets of sweat from her forehead. Toni is perspiring, too, though she feels far less elegant than Camille looks. The woman just has a knack for appearing classy at all times.

"It was good," Toni replies with a grin. "I mean, I think so. I was shaking like a leaf the whole time."

"No matter, dear. You'll get more comfortable as the evening goes on."

Camille is right about that. Three more *tandas* later and Toni's shaking has almost entirely receded. Her partners—another Argentine man named Juan who isn't quite strong enough to steer her around the floor properly, the Swede she danced with during the instructional period, and an Aussie with a roguish grin whose hand gets a little too close to her backside—have given her confidence that she's not the worst one in the room and that she's getting better with every step.

During the fourth break, Camille gives her a wink. "Choose your partner wisely," she advises. "This is the last one for us tonight."

"You won't hear me complaining," Toni laughs. "My feet are crying for an ice bath."

Camille grins and pats her on the thigh once more. Then, the bell rings out, and it is time for the final nerve-racking portion of the evening. As they've done four times already, the women stand and do the coquettish glancing to-and-fro that the *milonga* requires.

Toni feels Mateo searching her out. She considers it. He was nice, courteous, and handsome enough, plus a pleasant partner to dance with. But her eyes slide off him as if repelled by something invisible. She's not sure why. Maybe she just wants to explore as much as possible, rather than retreating to safe territory.

Or maybe, she realizes suddenly, it is because they are being drawn somewhere else.

She looks two feet to Mateo's left and locks eyes with the businessman from the airport. He is staring back at her with eyes like burning coals. She has a brief flashback to those eyes looking at her in the airport baggage claim area. Disdainful, haughty, condescending. The same level of intensity is there in his gaze now, too, but it has transformed into something altogether different.

Toni shivers. As before, it is as if she is being truly seen, skewered in place by this man's look. She feels a half dozen or more wild, unnamable emotions lurch upwards in her chest and decides to ignore them all because she doesn't know how to handle them.

She hasn't seen him since he entered the room earlier. She's been so focused on making sure she doesn't trip that she's hardly had time to look up. But the man's face makes her think that—maybe, just maybe —he's had his eyes on her the whole evening.

The businessman nods. It's a slow, careful nod.

And before she can think twice about it, Toni nods back.

The crossing of the dance floor towards him feels like it takes a lifetime. She slides past bodies on her right and on her left as folks make their introductions and prepare for the music to start.

The businessman hasn't taken his eyes off Toni. She takes him in once more while they approach each other. He is wearing gray suit pants with a subtle checkered pattern and a black belt to match his shoes. The crisp whiteness of his shirt stands out against his smooth, tanned skin. The cuffs on his sleeves are turned back just once, so she catches a glimpse of a sliver of muscular forearm.

And then he is in front of her, and she is in front of him, and it feels like all the sound in the room comes crashing in upon them like a wave in the ocean.

"I know you," she blurts.

He nods.

"From the airport," she explains clumsily. "With the bag, and, uh..."

He nods again. Toni falls silent.

"I am Nicolas," he says. She has to crane her neck a bit to look up at him—he's really tall. Up close and personal, she sees that he's quite broad, too. He must lift weights or something, going by how taut the fabric of his shirt is stretched across his chest and shoulders. His scent slices through the musk of the sweaty dancers thronged around them—sandalwood, sun-warmed leather, and a zest of citrus lingering on the edge of it all.

She realizes he is waiting for her to introduce himself. "Toni," she says simply.

She realizes also that he hasn't yet smiled or even threatened to do so. Why is she here? There were dozens of other men she could have danced with for this final section of music. So why did she choose this jerk? She feels a lash of irritation—at him, at herself.

"Would you like to dance with me, Toni?" he rumbles. He has a deep voice, one that she feels as much as she hears.

They've already done the nod-back-and-forth, so this verbal exchange feels superfluous. But there is a kind of subtext to it, Toni is noticing. She sees it in the way that Nicolas is looking at her, the way the corner of his lip is maybe leaning ever so slightly towards a wry grin, the way his hands are folded and clasped in front of his waist. She's not entirely sure yet what he's asking, and she's not entirely sure what to answer.

So she just nods. They step forward the last little bit. He's moving slowly, so Toni matches his speed. The world has shrunk down to just the two of them. His hand settles—one tiny point of connection at a time—between her shoulder blades. Even with just the weight of his fingertips on her back, Toni feels a sense of control radiating from him through her.

She reaches her own hand up and finds its resting place on the back of his shoulder. Under her palm, she feels his warmth, his strength. Their other hands clasp together in the empty space to their right, just as Toni's temple comes to nestle against the sharp line of Nicolas's jaw.

She closes her eyes and breathes. The music surges into rhythm.

And then they move.

It is immediately an entirely different experience than any of the dances she has done so far. Nicolas isn't yanking her around the floor as the Swede did, nor is he just trying to rub on her like the Aussie man had in mind.

But there is no doubt about who is leading the two of them. Nicolas's hand on Toni's back remains powerful, almost electric, and Toni finds herself drawing a kind of strength and guidance from it. It's easy to follow along with him, to match his steps with hers, his breath with hers, his warmth and pressure and heartbeat and vibration with hers.

His heartbeat thuds like a steel drum as the music ebbs and flows. Toni is terrified to open her eyes because she thinks that if she does, this will all turn out to be a strange dream. So she keeps them closed and finds that it doesn't matter if she does that, because Nicolas knows implicitly what she will do next. They step, step, step, side-step, drag together. Toni's hips move as they're meant to do without her even trying. Her whole body is coursing with a kind of tingling energy she has never known before. The dress, the music, his smell, his touch—it all weaves around her like a spell, and she lets herself be taken by it.

One song flows into the next, one step into the next. Before she knows it, the final note has rung out, and the dark, sensual drama of the music fades away, to be replaced by the rising murmur and laughter of the dancers as they peel themselves apart from one another.

But Nicolas doesn't let Toni go. For one tiny second longer than anyone else does with their partner, he holds onto her. Not crudely or rudely, but as if he is about to let go of something that he can never get back, and so he wants to savor it for a single moment more.

Then he releases her, and she wonders if she made that up.

"*Gracias,*" he rasps in a near-whisper.

Before she can say anything in response, he turns and leaves. Toni is left standing on the dance floor, still reeling from the beauty and power of whatever the heck just happened.

She's not sure how long she is standing stock-still before Camille comes up and taps her on the shoulder. She smiles brightly. "Did you have fun?"

Toni opens her mouth, then lets it fall closed again. Could what just happened be described as fun? Toni isn't sure. She's had fun before, and this wasn't quite that. She doesn't really have a word for it at all.

So she simply nods and smiles back at Camille.

"Excellent," the Frenchwoman says. "I am famished. Shall we find something to eat?" She doesn't wait for Toni's response. Instead, clutching Toni's elbow, she pilots the two of them out of the *milonga* and into the cool, crisp air of the Buenos Aires night.

# 5

ATLANTA, GEORGIA—JULY 1, 2000

After a while, Toni decided that she couldn't sit there any longer, in her car in the driveway of a house that wasn't hers anymore. She turned the key in the ignition, backed out, and headed down the road.

Just like the home she was leaving behind, her neighborhood now felt violated. Heather had driven down these roads with Toni's house and her husband in her sights. Had maybe waved hello to the elderly Keller couple, Mina and Lawrence, who lived at the corner. Or perhaps Heather had stopped to let Mrs. Nunez and her little schnauzer walk across the road.

Come to think of it, maybe Jared and Heather had been in her car together, laughing with the windows down and the music up and the wind tousling their hair. Maybe his hand was resting on her thigh. Maybe he'd opened the door for her and they'd fallen through it in each other's arms, kissing madly, clinging to one another greedily and recklessly.

The thoughts tumbling through her head one after the other made Toni nauseous. She thought for a moment that she would need to pull over, or else she would crash her vehicle.

She knew full well that she was rubbing salt in a wound that was still fresh and bleeding, but she couldn't stop herself from doing it anyway. So, in a last-ditch choice between crashing or crying, she chose the latter. She pulled into the as-yet-unfinished driveway of a house under construction and cried. Her tears plonked into her lap. It was a weirdly silent cry, a movie-star cry, not the boo-hoo, body-wracking sobs she might've expected.

Until, after a while, the tears stopped coming, as suddenly as if someone had turned off the faucet. In their place was a weird sort of humming, throbbing feeling, like when you've fallen asleep on your hand and aren't quite sure if it belongs to you anymore or not.

She was at a crossroads in her life; anyone could see that. The question was: *now what?*

Before she could decide, she was going to need some time to think. *Now what* was a big and scary question, and it presupposed an awful lot. Even acknowledging the question meant that she was giving up on Jared. Could her marriage be saved? She still had hope in her heart—what woman wouldn't?

But deep down in her bones, she knew that there was no chance of it. Jared had all but screamed it with his tepid "Yes, that's it." She wasn't quite ready to extinguish the flickering flame of hope she still safeguarded, but anyone could see that its time was running out.

So then, back to the question—now what?

There was only one real answer. Before Toni could fully process what she was doing, she had already picked up the phone and the line was ringing.

"Hello, this is the Benson residence, Mae speaking!" a familiar voice answered.

Toni took a deep sigh. She was just about to tell Mae everything that had happened because it felt all of a sudden like far too much for one person to bear all alone.

But before she could get the words out, she heard a shuffling, rustling kind of noise on the other end of the phone, and a low, laugh-tinged rumble saying, "Who's that, hummingbird?"

Mae shooed Henry away with a girlish chuckle as she shot back, "Well, how in heaven's name am I supposed to find out if you don't let me talk?" Clearing her throat, she then said back into the phone, "I'm sorry, dear, who did you say this was?"

Toni smiled bitterly. Glancing in the rear-view mirror, she saw that there was still one lone tear clinging to the tip of her nose. She swallowed and said in a bright, cheery voice that felt like it was a million miles away from the interior of this lonely car, "It's me, hon!"

"Toni! Hello, my love. How are you?"

"I'm great," Toni lied. "Calling with good news, actually."

"Oh? What's that?"

"I decided to come back home after all."

Mae chirped, "Wonderful! Oh, that is good news indeed. Everyone is going to be so excited to see you. As a matter of fact..." Toni heard Mae's breathing get a little fainter. She must be putting the phone down. She could just barely make out the muffled sound of her saying, "Brent, honey, come say hello to Aunt Toni!"

"You don't need to interrupt—" Toni started to protest.

But she didn't get to finish the thought before there was another rustle on Mae's end of the line, and a tinny voice called out happily, "Aunt T!"

"Hi, sweetness," Toni said. "How are you today?"

"Me and Daddy built the world's biggest sandcastle at the beach!" he bragged, sounding like it was the greatest accomplishment in the history of man. "It was as big as Daddy!"

"Oh my goodness," laughed Toni. "That sounds very big indeed."

"And then the waves came and whooshed it all away!" He added wave sound effects at the end.

"What an exciting day."

"It was the best day ever."

"I bet it was, honey."

He paused. "Are you coming for the Fourth of Joo-ly?" He pronounced the name of the holiday carefully, giving each syllable some time to breathe on its own.

Toni smiled. The tear still clung to the tip of her nose. "I think so," she said softly. "I would love to see you."

"Okay..." he said. His voice grew softer as he handed the phone back to his mom.

"Brent Benson!" Toni could hear Mae admonishing her youngest. "Come give your aunt a proper goodbye!"

"Bye, Aunt Toni!" called his pipsqueak little voice from far away. "I love you!"

"I love you, too, darling," she said back.

Mae sighed. "That boy is a Tasmanian devil," she said. In the background, Toni heard Brent roaring like a dinosaur. "I'm going to be gray in no time at all. Anyway, dear, what prompted the change of plans?"

Toni gnawed at her lip. A father and his young daughter wheeled slowly down the street on bicycles ahead of her. It was a pretty summer's day, sunlit and endless. "Jared got caught up with a work project. It could be a big client, so we decided to just do a rain check on the lake-house trip and save it for another time."

"I'm sorry to hear that. I know you were looking forward to it. But we're all thrilled to have you home for the holiday. Does that mean Jared won't be coming along for the ride?"

"No," Toni said. "No, Jared won't be there." It felt like a sentence that held far more significance than it might have seemed. Toni found it hard to speak out loud.

But Mae, as was her way, smoothed right over that with her trademark cheer. "A shame, of course, but like I said, we're happy to have you nonetheless. As a matter of fact, Henry just told me that he's been shanghaied into helping Mike Dunleavy at a fishing tournament out of town, so he's going to be gone for most of the weekend as well. The nerve of that man, I swear!"

"Now you see where Brent gets it from," Toni teased.

"That was never a mystery, I promise you that. Okay, well, yay! Ladies and the kids for the weekend. I'm excited already."

"Me too," Toni said quietly. "I think I could use a little time at home."

"Then come on home, darling. We'll be waiting."

They said their goodbyes and hung up the phone. As soon as Mae was gone, Toni felt like some of the warmth left the car. Even though it was a hot day in Georgia, there was a chill surging up and down her spine and along the backs of her legs.

She knew she was shutting the door on a part of her life, and she wasn't quite sure how she was meant to handle that. There ought to be some kind of ceremony or at least a moment of reflection to mark moving from one stage to another. Something better than Jared's feeble, "Yes, that's it." That didn't do the moment justice at all.

But what was a woman to do? She was now thirty-nine, single, childless, and probably homeless to boot. Her only immediate plans for the future were to fly to Nantucket and drink a large glass of wine, not necessarily in that order.

So, with the same tough-minded pragmatism that she had done everything else in her life, Toni Benson decided to heck with it—who needs a ceremony? Who needs a cheating husband? Who needs to cry? She put the car in drive and put her old life in the rear-view.

It was time to go home to Nantucket.

# 6

BUENOS AIRES, ARGENTINA—MAY 19, 2018

It has taken some time, but Toni is finally getting used to the bizarre hours by which the Argentines live their life.

Breakfast is always late, almost never before ten in the morning. And even then, it's hardly more than an espresso and something sweet to nibble on. The *porteños* do love their sweets, as it turns out (not that Toni is complaining about that!). *Medialunas*, the sweet and buttery Argentine riff on croissants, have quickly found their home in her heart.

Lunch, which comes much later in the afternoon as well, perhaps two or three, is also not much of a big eater's occasion. As it turns out, they save all their appetite for dinner, which is when the national palate truly shines.

By the time Toni gets to dinner each day—which is served anywhere from 10 p.m. all the way up to midnight—she is ravenous, *I-could-eat-a-cow* hungry. Fortunately, eating a cow is exactly what the whole country has in mind.

No matter where she goes to eat, the table is inevitably sagging with juicy, sizzling plates of the finest meat that she has ever tasted. *Asados, chorizo, mollejas, morcillas*—every cut and flavor imaginable, served alongside puréed potatoes and fresh, fragrant salads. Everything is washed down with copious glasses of rich red wine. It makes the long day of minimal-calorie consumption feel worthwhile to take that first, melt-in-your-mouth bite of steak and feel the tannins of the wine simmer like a mirage on her tongue.

That won't come until much later today, though. For now, she must content herself with a crisp, bitter espresso and the remains of her *medialuna*.

"Daydreaming again?" Camille asks from the other side of the table. They're seated nestled up against the window at a charming little café in San Telmo, the more bohemian section of the city. Toni has been idly watching the pedestrians go by and fantasizing about what dinner that night might present.

"Something like that," Toni answers with a soft smile. "Dreaming about something delicious."

"Or some*one* delicious, perhaps?" her friend teases.

Chuckling, Toni shakes her head immediately. "Who, me? Never. Not I."

But that's not entirely true. Because, in the two weeks since the tango class, Toni has thought more than once about Nicolas. She can't shake the bone-deep sensation that lingers from being led around the dance floor in his arms.

It wouldn't be quite right to call it a romantic feeling. It's more just that she has spent many, many years—ever since Jared, in fact—proving to herself that she is capable all on her own. As a result, the experience of surrendering completely to the touch and sway of another person is alien.

"Mhmm," Camille purrs, as though she doesn't believe Toni in the slightest. Camille made one or two comments about the night's array of partners after they left the *milonga*, but Toni didn't take any of that dangling bait. She merely laughed and said that it was a pleasant evening, but she was quite looking forward to a shower and bed. Back then, just as she is doing now, Camille merely *mhmm'd* and said nothing further.

"Cami..." Toni warns.

Camille holds her hand against her chest in mock offense. "Did I say a thing?"

"You said enough."

"I said nothing. Not even a word."

"Sometimes a noise is all it takes."

"You are paranoid, *cariño.*"

"'A paranoid is someone who knows a little of what's going on,'" Toni recites authoritatively.

"Is that a quote?"

"William S. Burroughs."

One of the strangest things thus far about Toni's experience in Argentina is the discovery that there is far more time in the day than she has ever realized before. In eighteen years of running the Sweet Island Inn, she never once went to bed with a perfectly complete task list. She always supposed that was the nature of being in the hospitality business—you were never going to get it all done. But it's now a bit disconcerting sometimes for Toni to look down at her dinner plate and realize that yet another day has whisked by and she has hardly noticed it.

So, in a strange way, this has been a retirement of a sort—although, whenever anyone she has met asks her if that's what has brought her here, she is adamant that it is merely a trip, not a retirement, and makes sure to throw in a little bit of haughtiness to that response, as if to make clear that she has no intention of throwing in the towel on her life.

But she cannot find the heart to complain about all this newly discovered time. Time to eat, time to relax, time to do nothing at all—and so much of it! She's at long last caught up on a reading list that was two decades old and a mile long.

She's also taken to writing down quotes from her books that she particularly likes. Camille may have begun rolling her eyes whenever Toni offers up a new proverb or beautiful turn of phrase, but there is something nice about finding a little gem of the English language when she is surrounded day and night by so much that she still does not fully understand.

That being said, her high school Spanish has come back faster than expected. With Cami's help, Toni has grown more and more confident at managing the little micro-interactions that life in a big city requires. Giving directions to the taxi driver, explaining her order to the man behind the counter at the butcher shop—bit by bit, Toni is finding her sea legs in the strange and wondrous ocean that is Buenos Aires.

The women sit in silence and sip their coffee for a little while. After a few minutes have passed, Camille turns back to Toni with a wicked gleam in her eye.

"So, tonight..." she begins.

"Oh no."

"No, no, no," Camille interrupts. "You want a quote, Toni? 'An open mind is like an open window: it lets the fresh air in.'"

Toni starts to argue, but she stops short of saying anything. Instead, she has a sudden and jarring flashback to the night she booked the flight to Argentina in the first place.

*Buenos Aires—the city of fair winds.*

Isn't that what she is seeking?

She slumps back into her seat, resigned. Camille smiles because she knows she's won. "And you will wear the red dress again, yes?" she asks.

"Who am I to argue?" Toni says with defeated sarcasm. "Your wish is my command."

Cami winks. "That's the spirit, *cariño*."

Which is how Toni finds herself seated in a wooden chair at the periphery of the *milonga* a dozen hours later. Her black heels are tapping on the dance floor with nervous energy, though she keeps her hands clasped together so they don't tremble too much.

Just as she did last time, Camille rests her hand on Toni's thigh and gives her a reassuring smile. "Ready?" she asks.

"As ready as I'll ever be."

"Your mystery man is not here, right?"

That, at least, is true. Nicolas is conspicuously absent. Toni scans the crowd, but she doesn't really need to. She has the sense that she would know the instant he entered the room, even if she were facing the opposite direction. Something about that confident, magnetic energy of his would vibrate through her like a struck bell.

"No," she answers softly. "All clear."

"Clear indeed," Camille responds. "So nothing to worry about, yes?"

"Why do I feel like we've had this conversation before?" Toni teases. "Déjà vu, I think you would call it."

Camille pretends to shudder. "Darling, you are an angel, but your French accent is in desperate need of work."

Despite the nerves she feels burbling below the surface, Toni laughs, and the two women settle into the kind of easy back-and-forth chatter that has marked their friendship since the moment they met.

Soon afterward, the bell dings, and the *milonga* begins. Toni finds herself dancing this first *tanda* in the arms of a strapping, burly older gentleman who went a little heavy on the cologne this evening.

She's surprised by how quickly she falls into the rhythm and grace of the movements. From the first crashing strings section flowing through the speakers into the spiky rise and fall of the music, she is smiling and striding confidently. The man she's with is a capable dancer, though he could look a little less dour. *It's a dance, not a funeral!* Toni nearly cries out to him jokingly.

But as soon as that thought crosses her mind, she thinks of her brother.

With a forceful wrench, she turns her mind back to the dance. But for the rest of the song, it keeps straying away. Back to Nantucket, to a fresh patch of grass and a gravestone she never thought she would have to see. Argentina has soothed away her pain like a mother laying her cool hand on the forehead of a child in bed with fever, but it's still there, ready to spring upon her when she least expects it.

Even now, as she is consumed by the smell of the man's cologne, the crescendo of each spicy, confident song, and the whirl of bodies pressing in around her on all sides, she can feel the grief eager to pounce and drag her into the shadowy corner where it lives.

She tries to smile through it. When the song ends, she shakes her partner's hand with a forced grin and retreats to her seat at the perimeter.

"That was dreadful," Camille says. She's wincing as she collapses into the seat next to Toni. "Like dancing with a drunken elephant."

Glancing down, Toni sees that there are already bruises blossoming on two of Camille's toes. "Yikes," she says distractedly.

Camille hears the warble in Toni's voice and glances up sharply. "*Cariño*, are you okay?"

"I'm—"

The sentence dies on her lips as the doors to the room are thrown open, and who should march in but Nicolas.

His suit tonight is a dark maroon, of all things. On any other man— or any other mannequin, even—it would look garish, borderline ridiculous. But Nicolas wears it well. He transforms it into something elegant and elusive. He's wearing a white shirt, as before, perfectly starched and open at the throat to reveal a flash of tan skin and a smattering of curled chest hair.

He pauses a step or two inside the door and locks eyes with Toni immediately. As if he knew she'd be here. As if he knew she'd be sitting in this chair, in this moment.

He doesn't smile or wave. He just nods, and his timing couldn't be more impeccable, because just then, the bell rings to signal the beginning of the next *tanda*.

For a moment, Toni considers refusing. It wouldn't be hard, after all. She could just let her eyes slide away and find someone else. The crowd is thick tonight, and she's already noticed more than one man eager to catch her attention. No doubt the red dress has something to do with that.

A weird thrill moves through her at the thought of refusing him. She thinks about doing just that. Finding someone else, and registering Nicolas's emotions as she does. Would he be angry? Amused? Indifferent? She's not sure which of those she'd prefer.

But she will never get to discover how Nicolas would react to her dismissal of him, because she finds herself nodding even before she's consciously decided to do so.

The moment between the nod and his approach feels like crossing an endless gulf. All around her, the bodies of the dancers are pairing off and finding their space in the *ronda*. Camille slinks into the arms of an impossibly tall fellow with a thick red beard and a glimmer in his eye.

But Toni barely notices all that. *You only have eyes for him*—that was a teasing thing her mother used to say whenever she caught teenage Toni with a crush on one of the neighborhood boys. It was just a turn of phrase, one of many little quirks her mother had. Toni never paid it much mind.

Now, though, she understands what it means. It's as if the rest of the world has faded into black and white, and the only thing left in full color is the man making his way through the crowd towards her. She reminds herself that she's still irritated at him, that being a good dancer does not absolve him of being a rude jerk, but repeating that mantra feels a bit like shouting into the wind of a hurricane, for all the good it does at turning away what is inevitably coming her way.

He pauses at the edge of the dance floor and extends a broad hand towards her. "Toni," he says. It's a greeting, an invitation, a recognition, and a million other things less specific, but all the more tantalizing for it, bundled together into one word. No one has ever said her name quite that way. As with everything about this man, she cannot decide whether or not she likes it.

She steps forward and takes his hand. Neither of them takes their eyes off each other as they assume their place in the rotation. Toni is suddenly finding it hard to breathe as Nicolas's palm slides up and settles in the middle of her back, strong and assured.

Her hand comes to rest lightly on the bunched muscle at the back of his shoulder, as before. And their right hands clasp together, hovering in the air.

Toni studies Nicolas's face. She wants to find answers. Why did he come here? Was it for her? If so, why? She is a fifty-seven-year-old woman with a life full of stumbles behind her and a very uncertain future ahead of her. What could he see in her?

And what could she see in him? As far as she knows, he is a rude businessman of some kind who walks into every room like he owns it. That's the beginning and end of their relationship. She tells herself that she's making much ado about nothing. He liked dancing with her, and she with him, and there's no need to build a mountain from such an inconsequential little molehill.

But she can see in the clench of his jaw and the curve of his eyebrow that that's not right. There is more here, though it remains as yet unspoken. And even if she doesn't know what to make of that, she's certain it is still true.

She closes her eyes and sighs. This is overwhelming. For a moment, she even considers stepping away, going outside, and just walking until these confusing thoughts are left behind her. But then the music strikes its first chord, and the window of opportunity to do that slams shut.

Nicolas strides once and coaxes her along with him. She steps in time with him, and then they do it again, and again, melded together chest to chest. His eyes never leave hers. She feels the pressure of his hand on her back slowly assert itself. And, as before, his smell invades her nostrils. It is the same scent as it was the first time they danced— sandalwood, leather, and citrus, a smell that has instantly become one and the same as Nicolas himself, such that if she ever smelled it wafting on a breeze, she would turn to try and find him, no matter how many miles or years removed from this moment she might happen to be.

As they move together, Toni feels a deluge of emotions and sensations paired together that make no sense. She feels ethereal and incredibly solid at the exact same time, so raw with an incomprehensible surge of hot feeling that she can feel a blush rising to her cheeks at the thought of other people seeing her do this out here in the open, with this stranger, this man, this—whatever he is becoming to her.

When the *tanda* ends, the blush lingers. Toni brushes back a strand of hair that has fallen over her forehead and glances down at her feet in something akin to embarrassment. She forces herself to look up again a moment later, as much as she would prefer not to, and meet Nicolas's eyes once again.

"You have a natural elegance," he says. The words are nice, but the way he says it is flat and roughshod, as if he doesn't care one way or the other whether she finds his comment complimentary or not. Again, that familiar half irritation, half flirtation feeling churns in her chest.

"My ex-husband would disagree with you," she says. She has a sudden memory of Jared's face, twisted in anger, on a night when she accidentally stumbled and dropped a serving tray with their dinner on it. She was laughing before the plates hit the ground. But Jared didn't laugh.

"Perhaps that is why he is no longer your husband, then," Nicolas muses with a wry twinkle in his eye.

Toni chuckles. Though random memories of Jared still flash up like old aches from time to time, she feels for the most part like her life with him was eons ago. He doesn't have quite the same hold over her heart that he once did. "That among many, many other reasons."

Nicolas nods knowingly. "When someone tells you who they are, believe them."

"Go tell that to young Toni."

"Young Nicolas could do with hearing that himself," the man laughs.

Toni raises an eyebrow. "Oh?"

"I have an ex-wife," he explains. "I would say it is water under the bridge, but that would be a lie. Children make it hard to say such things."

"That they do." Toni isn't sure where she ought to let Nicolas's comment settle in her mind. She feels, as she always does, that familiar pang she gets whenever someone mentions children. It's like the ghost of how badly she wanted a child, back in the Jared days, still haunts her and twists the knife when she least expects it.

On a completely different level, the thought of this gruff, serious-looking man playing with children feels wildly incongruous. If she'd had to guess, she would've said he was the kind of man who preferred to ignore children altogether whenever possible. Wrong on that count, she supposes.

"How many children do you have?" she asks politely. Around them, the hubbub of folks looking for their next partners provides an easy backdrop to their conversation, like listening to a little brook in the woods chortle as it rounds the bend.

"Just one. A girl. That was more than enough, I assure you."

"Girls are tough."

"You don't even know the half of it. Do you have a daughter as well?"

Toni gnaws at her lip. "No," she answers finally. "I don't have any children." The ghost twists the knife another notch.

"Well, they are tough. She is why I am here, actually. She's getting married soon, and I cannot embarrass myself with a poor tango at her wedding."

Toni arches an eyebrow quizzically. "You don't seem like you need much practice."

He grins, and for a moment, Toni would've almost called it a sheepish grin before it shifts into the familiar taunting, almost arrogant grin she is used to seeing on him. "I needed the practice last week. I confess, I came here this week with somewhat of a different agenda."

"What's that?"

"To dance with you again, of course. And then to ask if you would like to get a drink with me."

Toni is flabbergasted, to say the least. Sure, their quasi-adversarial relationship has had some flirtatious back-and-forthness to it. And sure, she's noted to herself on numerous occasions that Nicolas is quite attractive. But the open-faced directness with which he just asked the question has taken her by surprise. She's been quick to assume that he's just a jerk, and any passing spark between them is accidental at best. Perhaps, though, it has just been that she forgot a simple truth about human nature that even children know: sometimes the meanest boy on the playground, the one who pulls your pigtails the hardest, is really the one who likes you the most.

"I...I..."

"Have I overstepped?" Nicolas asks, with that same twinkle glistening in his eye. He's half daring, half concerned that she might actually turn him down. He is clearly not a man who is used to being told no.

"No," Toni answers in the end. "I...Yes, I would be happy to get a drink with you."

"Fantastic. I have to travel for work this week. Perhaps next weekend, then?"

"Yes," Toni says, nodding distantly as if she's in a dream, "that sounds good."

He pulls a business card from his pocket and hands it to her with an apologetic shrug of the shoulders. "I'm sorry if this seems oddly formal," he says, "but it is all I have."

Toni takes it from him, not failing to notice that their fingers brush past each other as Nicolas hands the card over, and looks down at it. *Nicolas Perez*, it says. *Owner/Dueño, Perez Internacional.* "Did you just give this to me so I'd see that you were the boss?"

To her surprise, Nicolas blanches. "Of course not," he says in horror.

"I'm kidding," she interjects before he has a conniption. She realizes suddenly that she's reached out and laid her fingertips to rest reassuringly on his forearm. They linger for longer than they ought to, and when she pulls them away, they tingle.

"Oh," he says. Then his face splits in a genuine smile. "I thought you might...never mind."

The sudden modesty is unexpected, but cute, in its own way. They stand still for a second and look anywhere but at each other, as eye contact would suddenly be too much to bear.

What Toni can't get over is that her stomach is suddenly filled with the kind of nervous, excited butterflies she thought she'd experienced the last of more than thirty years prior. Women her age aren't supposed to go on first dates. Women her age aren't supposed to flirt with strange men. Right?

Wrong.

Because women her age also aren't supposed to wear gorgeous red dresses and go dance the way she and Nicolas just did. Women her age don't board planes to foreign countries on one-way tickets, sequestering away hope that the world is both bigger and more beautiful than they might've dared to dream of before.

But Toni has done those things, and then some. So maybe she can do other things that women her age are not supposed to do.

Her heart still hurts. It may never stop hurting. But perhaps she is more than the woman she thought she was. And perhaps this is the universe's way of shoving that truth in her face.

"I'll see you next week, Nicolas," she says with a smile. She winks and turns, still holding his business card in her hand. This time, she is the one who leaves him standing speechless.

It feels good.

# 7

ATLANTA, GEORGIA—JULY 1, 2000

By the time Toni pulled into the long-term parking section of the Atlanta airport, she was feeling far better than she might have expected.

This was the real her—a doer, an action-taker. Antonia Evelyn Benson did not wallow in her self-pity. Her mother would roll over in her grave if she'd ever caught Toni doing something so pathetic as crying over a man who surely did not deserve her.

That thought was the first thing that had made Toni smile. Angeline, her mom, was a tour de force if ever there was one. She was the source of much of Toni and Henry's fiery elements. Their dad had provided more of the calming, mellow influence on their personalities.

It was funny how, even nearly a decade since her passing, Toni could hear her mother's voice in her ear. *Antonia Benson, you quit that crying right now, young lady!* she would've barked. Mom had a husky, raspy voice that she always hated, but Toni had loved it. It felt musty, familiar, like the smell of a blanket you'd had your whole life. She would've committed acts of treason right now in exchange for one more cup of tea with Mom at the kitchen table. That table was Mom's domain—bills and papers stacked everywhere, legal pads filled to the margins with her elegant longhand, and an ever-present cup of tea at her side.

Toni closed her eyes and pictured settling into a seat at the table across from her. Mom would've fixed her with a glare over those glasses she wore to read—"my old-lady glasses," as she called them. It wasn't an unkindly glare, per se, but rather the kind of glare that says, *You already know what I'm going to tell you.*

*"My heart hurts, Mom,"* Toni would've told her.

*"For what?!"* would've been the immediate response, bordering on indignant. *"For a man who stole twelve years of your life?"*

*"For the marriage that fell apart. For the kids I don't have. For the life I thought I was supposed to be living. I don't know. All of it, I guess."*

And then, that wise cackle. The *you-don't-know-a-darn-thing* cackle. Mom was always the best at that.

*"Child, if you think your life is over now, then I have some news about the next forty to fifty years. Your time isn't up, honeysuckle, not by a long shot."*

That felt absurd. Who starts over at thirty-nine? No fairy tales start with a woman who's already had a hot flash or two.

But in her mind's eye, Toni saw her mother's all-knowing grin, and it was impossible to argue with.

And so, as she put her ticket on the dashboard and turned her eyesight towards the terminal, she felt her chin rising a little higher with every step. Her breath came easier. It didn't feel quite so much anymore like someone was pressing down on her chest with a heavy fist, squeezing the air out of her.

She was going home to Nantucket. She was going to see Mae and Henry and the kids; that was always a shot of life. Smelling the ocean breeze and basking in the sunshine that she knew and loved—how could this not be a good thing?

While she was home, she would take the time to take stock of her life, her past and future alike. Maybe there was a chance at saving everything with Jared. If he apologized and explained himself, she could find a way to move past things, right? All she'd ever wanted was for him to love her. All she'd ever wanted was to make him happy. That hadn't changed yet, had it? It was impossible to say, and she was still far too close to it. Going home would give her the distance she needed to make decisions.

She passed through security and moved down the massive corridors. She found a seat outside her gate and settled in, feeling ready for—well, ready for whatever was next. Then that feeling came to an abrupt halt.

"Toni?" someone gushed from behind her.

Toni turned around in her seat and saw a familiar face ogling her. "Hello, Lisa."

Lisa Garvey came around the row of seats and enveloped Toni in a big, mushy hug. She was a lot of woman in every sense of the word. Wide, tall, with huge, bottle-blonde Southern curls, acres of gaudy jewelry on her ears and wrists, and enough perfume to knock out a buffalo. But she had the personality to match—sweet as pie with a booming laugh, and bubbly enough to talk your ear off if you gave her the runway. She was the kind of woman you were glad to see at a party if you didn't know anyone else there.

"Hon, you look trim! Have you been working out? I bet you're one for hot yoga; that's got Toni Benson written all over it."

Toni blushed. "A little of this, a little of that," she mumbled, caught off guard.

Lisa gave her a playful swat on the shoulder. "What're you doing at an airport when I don't know about it?"

Lisa was a travel agent, and she'd been booking trips for Jared and Toni for almost six years now. Barbados a few years back for a winter getaway, a ski trip to Vail, a weekend escape to the Grand Canyon so Toni could check it off her bucket list. The job suited her —she liked knowing what people were doing, circulating folks around the country and around the world and living vicariously through them.

"A little trip home," Toni said briefly, hoping Lisa wouldn't press further, even as she knew that it was inevitable.

"Bringing that scoundrel husband of yours to see the family, then? Where is that ragamuffin?" She made a show of looking around. No doubt she expected Jared to come around the corner any minute.

But when he didn't show, her eyes settled back on Toni, and she frowned a bit.

"Jared is, uh..." Toni began awkwardly. She didn't know where to start or what to share. She just knew that she felt foolish for ever feeling like things were going to be okay. Here she was at the first hurdle in her newly single life, and she was making a fool of herself already. Surely she should've expected that she would have to explain to someone sooner or later what had happened? Perhaps it was the suddenness of this encounter that was throwing her for a loop, or maybe she really had been praying that everyone would magically forget that Jared had ever existed and she'd never have to explain his whereabouts to anyone.

"I'm asking because I wouldn't have thought you'd book two trips so close together!" Lisa exclaimed, chuckling her way out of the uncomfortable moment.

Toni wrinkled her nose. "Two trips? What do you mean?"

Lisa spread her arms wide. Her jewelry clacked together as she said, "Paris, love! He told me it wasn't a surprise, so I don't feel guilty sharing it with you, but that hubby of yours just booked a trip for two to Paris. Next weekend, as a matter of fact, assuming I don't have my wires crossed."

No one's heart had ever plummeted as quickly or as cruelly as Toni's did just then. It felt like it dropped straight into the pit of her stomach and imploded on contact.

*A trip for two to Paris.*

Jared was never going to bring her on that trip. It was for him and Heather. Toni felt nauseous, dizzy, and slightly crazed, like she was maybe about to tear her hair out and start running around the airport terminal, screaming nonsense at the top of her lungs. This wasn't an accident. It wasn't a casual fling gone wrong. This was a planned betrayal.

That didn't hurt her any more or less, but it registered with a dull, emotionless thud. She looked up at Lisa, who was still regarding her with a look of curiosity in her eye.

"I, uh… Excuse me for a sec, I need to go to the restroom." Toni didn't wait for an answer.

As she scurried away and tried to hide the tears welling in her eyes, she heard Lisa calling over, "Er, well, my flight's boarding, love! It was so good to see you! Bon voyage!"

Toni just kept going.

She flew into the bathroom, into an empty stall, and locked the door behind her. Then, sinking onto a seat on the toilet, she let loose tears that had been building up, one at a time, for the last twelve years.

She cried for what she'd once had and didn't have anymore. She cried for what she'd never have and would never have again. She cried and cried, and she didn't feel much better when she finished crying, so she just started all over and kept crying some more.

Forty-five minutes passed like that. She heard her mom's voice in her ear again—*What's worth crying for, honeysuckle?*—but it didn't comfort her this time. It just made her miss her mom on top of everything else.

She forced herself to get to her feet, though she had to stick a hand out to lean against the wall for support since her legs had fallen asleep. Then, limping uncomfortably, she washed her hands and rinsed her face before exiting the bathroom.

She was just in time to hear groans rise up from the small crowd assembled in front of her gate. *DELAYED* read the small TV screen embedded in the wall above the check-in counter.

"Excuse me," she said to a frumpy-looking woman with a scowl on her face. "Did I miss an announcement?"

"Flight's not happening tonight," the woman spat in disgust. "Plane trouble, or so they say. We ain't leavin' 'til tomorrow mornin'."

Toni did the only thing she could do: she laughed. The frumpy woman gave her a suspicious side-eyed look, tucked her child behind her legs, and shuffled away, never taking her eyes off Toni.

But Toni didn't care. What could there possibly be left to care about? She was caught no matter which way she turned. Caught on the ugly end of a loveless, unfaithful marriage; caught on the wrong side of a biological clock that wouldn't stop ticking for anybody; and now, she was caught in the Atlanta airport. At least until the morning.

She collected her things and found a small restaurant tucked in a quiet corner of the airport. She ordered a margarita that she didn't drink and a cold sandwich she didn't eat. Mostly, she just sat and stared at the back of her hands, wondering if she was imagining wrinkles or if they were really starting to appear.

She couldn't say for sure whether she was being hysterical or if her mood was justified. She knew only that her mother would disapprove of it, and so she tried to chin up and remind herself that Nantucket wasn't so far or so long away. Soon enough, she'd be able to mush her toes into the sand and turn her face to the wind. And even if the world wouldn't change, she knew that there was a tiny shred of peace that could be snatched in that moment. She just had to get there.

The airport gradually emptied of people as night fell. When the restaurant closed up shop, Toni found an out-of-the-way chair not too far from her gate, fashioned a makeshift pillow out of a garment in her suitcase, and curled up to go to sleep.

She didn't dream at all.

# 8

BUENOS AIRES, ARGENTINA—MAY 26, 2018

Toni comes out of the shower to find that she has a missed call on her cell phone. She picks it up to see who rang and smiles when she sees the name. She dials the number back immediately.

"Hello?" Mae answers.

"You have no idea how lovely it is to your voice, darling," Toni says at once.

"As lovely as it is to hear yours, I'm sure!"

Toni is a little surprised by the intensity of the feeling she's swimming in all of a sudden—a feeling of longing, deep and desperate, with a kind of wistful fondness woven through it.

Perhaps she has been lonelier than she allowed herself to realize. Buenos Aires has been wondrous, and Camille has been as pleasant a companion as she could ask for. But at the end of the day, nothing fills that space in your heart quite like home. And Mae's voice is nothing if not home. Like Henry, she *is* Nantucket, as far as Toni is concerned. She is white sand beaches and stoic lighthouses and fresh-caught lobster and clean linens blowing in the summer breeze.

"How're things?" Toni blurts before she accidentally starts waxing poetic and frightens Mae into thinking she is having a psychotic meltdown half the world away.

"Now, now, hold your horses," Mae scolds, "I'm not the one on an international adventure! How are *you*?"

Toni smiles. "It has been an interesting couple months, that is for sure."

"If you think you're going to get away with a pitiful little answer like that, you've got another thing coming. Come, come now, tell me everything!"

"Just tell me where you are first," Toni says. Apparently, she's going to wax poetic after all. "Describe it to me. I honestly think I'm starting to forget what home looks like."

She can hear Mae smiling through the phone. "I suppose I can do that. It's funny you should ask, actually; I just sat down on the porch out back. It is a morning so beautiful that I ought to try bottling it up just so I can save it for a rainy day. I've got a cup of hot coffee in hand, all the guests have gone out to town or to the beach already, and my task list is mercifully short. The only thing missing is a kind face to fill the seat next to me."

Toni smiles once more, and when she reaches a hand to her face, it comes away wet. Only then does she realize she's crying. It's not a sad cry or a bitter one. It's something not so serious at all, she thinks. Just her body's way of telling her that her heart has never left the Sweet Island Inn.

"You don't even know how wonderful that sounds."

"Oh, I think I've got some idea, dear." She takes a sip of her coffee and *ahh*s contentedly. "Now, are you going to make me pin you down and pry your side of things out of you? My goodness, you're worse than Brent at bath time. I'm dying for a snippet of something exotic!"

"Where do I even begin, Mae?" Toni muses. She's lying on her back on the hotel bed, hair still wet from the shower and spread out across the top of the comforter. The fan overhead is beating lazily, and even though she just woke up a little while ago, she's already entertaining ideas of falling asleep again just like this, with Mae's voice murmuring into her ear. If she listens hard, she just might be able to hear the staticky sighs of the Nantucket ocean waves. "Let's see..."

She truly doesn't know where to begin, so she glances out of her window and just starts there. She tells Mae about how the city looks at sunrise, baking beneath a warm egg-yolk sun. How it looks faded and fresh all at once like someone carved each of the buildings from butter and then left them to slowly melt down together in beautiful dribbles and globs.

She tells her about the food, how the sidewalks are sizzling with the sound of open *asados* and how rich the coffee is and how delicious the wine tastes.

She tells her about the people, how they laugh and touch each other on the elbow and the shoulder when they're talking. How kind they are, and how beautiful, how proud.

"It's like—you're going to think I'm crazy—but it's like they found themselves in this warm, cozy, kind of turbulent but out of the way fork in a river, and instead of flowing downstream with the rest of the world, they decided to just stay there and put down roots." Toni feels herself blushing. "I'm sorry if that sounds absurd. I've been reading a lot of books lately, and I think I'm starting to fancy myself more artistic than I really am."

"Oh, don't be silly," Mae snaps good-naturedly. "That sounds absolutely beautiful. We miss you here, of course, but it sounds like you are living in quite a fairy tale."

"Complete with a handsome prince..." Toni teases.

She can practically hear Mae's eyebrows shoot up. Thankfully, all she says is, "Oh?"

"Well, not exactly. Mostly joking. Honestly, nothing of the sort," Toni backpedals as fast as she can. "Just, uh, getting drinks tonight with a... with a someone."

"What kind of someone are we talking, darling?"

"Just a friend, that's all."

"Mm. Well, friends are good."

Toni wants to laugh out loud—that's such a Mae answer. She knows that her sister-in-law wants to poke more, but she's never been pushy.

"Anyway," Toni says, fighting back the rising blush in her cheeks, "what's new on your end of the planet?" It's an obvious deflection, but she hopes Mae forgives her for it.

"A little of this, a little of that, but not really much of anything," Mae offers. She rattles off some minor changes to the inn's layout and a funny anecdote about a few of the guests from the last two months. "...But things are running smoothly, I promise."

"Of course they are," Toni replies. "You were cut out for this, that's for sure. I can't thank you enough. What about the kids?"

"The kids..." Mae whispers. Her voice has darkened suddenly.

Toni swallows hard. That doesn't sound good.

"The kids are okay," she concludes finally.

She gives a brief rundown on what everyone is doing: Eliza and Sara are harboring at home from some unspecified personal dramas, Holly and her husband are on shaky ground, and Brent is faring worst of all.

Even with her skipping over most of the details, it's clear to Toni that this is a tough topic of conversation for Mae. So, after offering condolences and her support, Toni decides to move along.

"And how are *you*, Mae?"

Mae pauses. "I'd be lying if I said I wasn't terribly sad a lot of the time. Nights are the hardest. I'm so grateful that I have the inn to keep me busy while the sun's up. And I'm so tired by the time I get to bed each day that I don't linger long before I fall asleep. But that little time that I am awake and alone...it hurts an awful lot, Toni."

Toni finds herself nodding in the silence of her hotel room. The fan overhead is lulling her towards sleep. She bites at her lip.

If only there were something to say to bundle up the sadness weighing on her and Mae like sandbags and toss it overboard. She knows there's no such thing—Lord knows it took her long enough to leave the grief of Jared behind—but it doesn't keep her from racking her brain, trying to think of something suitable nonetheless.

In the end, all she offers is a heartfelt, "I'm sad too, Mae. I don't think I'll ever stop being sad." She hopes that is enough. The thought of her sweet sister-in-law straining under the weight of such unexpected sorrow is heart-wrenching.

But that is life, isn't it? Minor miracles and wordless tragedies and the ebb and flow of all of those things. Life comes in seasons, in tides, and you just have to learn to tread water when the tide is high and head for shore when it's low enough to let you go. And, as she's learning, it's easier when you have a swimming buddy.

The two women sit in silence for a while, just listening to each other sigh. They talk a bit more after that, mostly idle tidbits about the comings and goings of the inn and Toni's life in Buenos Aires, and then Toni can feel the conversation headed towards its natural end.

"Well, tell the kids I love them very much," Toni says. "I love you, hon."

"I will, Toni. Love you too."

Toni is about to hang up when Mae adds, "Oh, and Toni?"

"Yes?"

"Be nice to the handsome prince, okay? Henry wouldn't want you to run the poor man off."

Toni doesn't know whether she wants to laugh or cry. In the end, she does a little of both, chuckling as another stray tear escapes down her face. "I'll do my best," she says.

"That's all any of us can ever do, darling. I'll talk to you soon. Take care."

They hang up. Toni marinates in the quiet for a little while. Then she coaxes herself to her feet to get dressed and go run a few errands she has on her plate for the day.

It feels good to move throughout the city with confidence. She navigates the subway and the lines at the grocery store and has a peaceful lunch to herself in a quiet poet's café in San Telmo. Her sadness slinks away for a while, thank goodness.

By the time she gets back home to her hotel room, she has just enough time to shower once more, change, and get ready.

Tonight, she is getting drinks with Nicolas.

~

"*Ciao*, Toni. You look stunning."

Toni blushes at once, as if she were fifteen years old and this was the first man to ever hit on her. "Hi, Nicolas."

He's standing at the corner of the bar, which is located in, of all things, a flower shop. Toni would've never thought to marry the two things together, but to her surprise, it works with stunning effect.

The lighting along the long, curved wall that runs down the right-hand side of the place is a warm amber that takes the chill from her bones. (She's still having trouble reconciling with the fact that, down here below the equator, July falls in the dead of winter.) The bar, done up in a pleasing blonde wood with white-backed chairs to match, runs parallel along the length of the whole space. And everywhere she looks, there are massive bouquets of flowers in every variety imaginable. The blooming bursts of color offer a delightful fragrance, as well as some privacy between seats at the bar and the booths scattered throughout.

The bartender comes over to speak to Nicolas. As the two of them converse in a quick blitz of Spanish, Toni takes the chance to look over her date while he's not paying attention.

She made him swear during their brief text exchange earlier in the week that he wouldn't dress over the top and make her feel like a bum. Apparently, he interpreted that as "don't wear your suit jacket," but has otherwise done nothing different than all the other times she's seen him.

Tonight's suit pants are a pale gray with the faintest powder blue pinstripes running through it, barely visible to the casual onlooker. As with all things related to fashion and Nicolas, it would look absurd on anyone else. But something about the gravitas that rolls off him makes the whole ensemble work.

The shirt he's wearing is a friendly blue that matches the pinstripe. He's got the cuffs rolled back to the elbow, showing off his lean forearms. The whole effect is of class, elegance, and something a little bit foreign that Toni just can't quite put her finger on.

As part of their pact not to dress up, Toni told Nicolas that she was just going to fish any old something out of her suitcase. But she took one look at the options she had available in her bags and decided she'd rather show up in a potato sack than wear any of that.

So, as part of her errands, she ducked into a few different boutiques she'd seen around town and ended up with a knee-length cardigan in tan faux fur to wear over a cozy white turtleneck and black jeans. She paired it with her favorite black leather booties.

Camille sent an approving thumbs-up when Toni told her what she planned on wearing. But even still, she felt a little nervous warble in her throat when she did one last twirl-and-examine in the bathroom mirror before leaving her hotel room.

She is here now, though, and there is no turning back. The bartender nods as the two men finish their conversation, and then Nicolas swivels his gaze over to Toni approvingly and smiles. "Would you like to find a booth?" he asks her.

She nods. "That'd be lovely, thanks."

Nicolas gestures for her to go ahead of him. They make their way to the back of the bar, with his hand hovering protectively over her mid-back.

The physical intimacy feels familiar already after their sessions at the *milonga,* but in this setting, it still manages to send a shiver racing down Toni's spine. She has the same thought she's been having again and again since—well, since she left Nantucket, really: *Aren't I too old for all this?* Too old to travel, to dance, to flirt, to buy new clothes and check herself out in the mirror while wondering what a handsome man will think of her?

And then, apropos of nothing, she imagines Henry laughing in the corner. *You crazy old coot!* he'd be cackling. *We're spring chickens, sis! Have a drink for me, okay?*

He is gone as suddenly as he came, but there is a warm feeling left behind, like the glow that lingers after a good laugh. She is still smiling as she settles into the booth across from Nicolas.

"Is something funny?" Nicolas asks wryly.

"Oh no, just a—too hard to explain, I think."

"I see. A woman of secrets."

"Says a very secretive man."

"How so?"

"The suits, the dancing, the..." She waves a hand to encompass him from head to toe. "All of it, you know. The aura."

"I think you have misunderstood me greatly. I am an open book, *bella.*"

Toni laughs at that. "I have been reading a lot of books since I got here, and I can assure you that you are far from open."

Nicolas's face—freshly shaven, she notes, though there seems to be no banishing the five o'clock shadow that lives perpetually on his jaw —breaks into a quizzical grin. "Would you like to play a game, then?"

"Oh dear. I have a bad feeling about this."

"Bah, no need. It is simple: you ask me a question, and I will answer. Then I will do the same for you."

They keep their eyes locked as a barback brings over their drinks and sets them down on a platter.

"I took the liberty of ordering for you," Nicolas explains when Toni arches an eyebrow at the murky concoction being set in front of her. "It is a staple of my country. You cannot leave without trying it."

"What on earth is it?" She examines the glass. It looks carbonated, with an inviting golden foam across the top.

"*Fernet con coca,*" Nicolas answers, pronouncing the words reverently like they're a national treasure.

"Come again?"

"Fernet branca and Coca Cola. I would explain it, but you really need to experience it for yourself."

She's hesitant. "When in Rome, right?" Before she can lose her nerve, she lifts the fizzing glass to her lips and takes a sip. Nicolas watches her carefully.

She starts coughing immediately. "Oh goodness, that is atrocious," she scowls. She sets the glass down and dabs at her lips with one of the white cloth napkins from the tabletop. "That tastes like someone dumped sugar into cough syrup."

Nicolas bursts out laughing. It's strange to see, like watching a dog suddenly start walking on its back legs. But it's not an unpleasant sight. He looks calmer when he laughs.

"You ought to do that more," she says when he has quieted down again.

"Do what?"

"Laugh."

He starts to say one thing, then changes tack halfway through. "You are an interesting woman, Toni."

"Not half as much as you seem to think," she fires back. "An interesting woman would probably like this drink."

"You are all the more interesting for not liking it," he insists. "Or at least, for telling me that you don't."

Toni feels a pang of guilt. Surely her parents raised her with better manners than that, didn't they? But there is something about Nicolas that tugs the truth out of her before she even has the chance to consider demurring politely. It's a bolder, more aggressive Toni who has come to get drinks with this man tonight. She's still not sure what to make of that.

"So, shall we play our game?" she answers. Anything to relieve the pressure that seems to be growing with each silent passing second.

"You don't like talking about yourself, do you?" Nicolas says instead of replying to her directly.

"Is that your first question?"

He grins. "I suppose it can be."

She weighs the question for a moment. "No," she says after thinking about it. "I guess I don't."

"Why not?"

"Ah, ah, ah," she tuts. "That's two questions. You can't take my turn so easily."

He raises his hands in surrender. "Fair is fair. I cede the floor."

She doesn't know quite where to start with this enigma of a man, so she picks a simple question to begin. "Where did you learn to speak such good English?"

"I travel a lot for work," he explains. "I run a shipping company, so my job takes me all around the world. I have spent a fair amount of time in your United States. Quite a country."

"How so?"

This time, he waggles his finger and smiles. "Now look who is trying to take two turns in one!"

"All right, all right," she chuckles. "You go on, then."

"Why don't you like talking about yourself, Toni?"

She feels equal parts defiant and embarrassed at the question. Why, in fact, doesn't she? It's easy enough to concede that it's true; she's always been more comfortable out of the spotlight. But why is that?

"I guess..." she starts, then stops. "Maybe it's...I just have always taken care of others, I think. I have a younger brother. *Had,* I should say." She winces and keeps going, hoping that Nicolas didn't notice the tense change and realizing that of course he noticed it. "And a husband, now ex. And an inn, with guests coming and going all the time. It's just what I've done, I think, for as long as I can remember. I'd rather hear about other people."

Nicolas nods. She wonders if he's going to say something, try to psychoanalyze her or whatever. But, mercifully, he says nothing. He just regards her with those gray eyes. They don't feel as cold as they once did, though the sharpness of their perception hasn't diminished.

The silence compounds on itself until it feels too heavy to bear. Toni stammers and fumbles for a question. "What is your daughter's name?"

"Isabella," Nicolas answers smoothly. "She will be twenty-four at the end of the year."

"Isabella," repeats Toni. "That is a lovely name."

"Thank you. She is a lovely woman." Again, just like with the laughter, it is somewhat bizarre to see a father's pride beaming in the face of this man. Maybe it's because Toni can't shake the memory of the condescension that Nicolas regarded her with when they first encountered each other at the airport. Or maybe it's because all of this—this bar, this man, this dynamic—feels like unfamiliar territory, though she can't say whether it feels like that because she's never been here before or simply because it's been so long since she has.

"My turn again?"

Toni nods, not quite trusting her voice.

"What is your home like?"

She tilts her head to the side. "That's an odd question."

"There is much to learn about a person from learning of their home."

"Right. Um, let's see. It's beautiful. I'm from Nantucket, a little island off the coast of Massachusetts, in the northeast United States."

"I know of it," Nicolas says with a *don't-mistake-me-for-stupid* kind of grin.

"Ah. Well, anyway, it's gorgeous."

"You have to give me more than that, surely."

Toni racks her brain. Home feels so very far away all of a sudden. Mae's description of the sun rising over the inn's porch during their call this morning comes to mind. She closes her eyes for a moment and tries to picture it. Standing on the front porch of the Sweet Island Inn and looking outward...now, it begins to unfold in her mind's eye like a picture book. She can see it, sense it, smell it.

She opens her eyes. "It's like...There's...well, let's see. Where to begin? There's Winter Stroll, and when the snow falls, it's like living in a snow globe, this perfect little Hallmark town with hot chocolate and the most beautiful art on display, and Christmas trees lit up like constellations. And in the summer, the breeze is just about the freshest thing a man or woman could ever hope to smell, and the sun is so lovely that a nap on the porch feels darn close to heaven. And the, the...Oh dear, I am rambling like a fool."

She's taken note of Nicolas's smile, which has softened into something affectionate and cautious, like a husband watching his wife sleep and being careful not to disturb her.

"What?" she snaps self-consciously.

"You love your home."

"Yes," Toni replies softly. "I do."

"I can see it in you."

"What else can you see in me, Dr. Freud?" she teases. Again, she'll say anything to lighten the pressure of Nicolas's stare. It's making her feel —well, *hot and bothered* is what a person of her generation might say.

"You shouldn't joke about that. We Argentines take psychotherapy very seriously."

"Is that a fact?"

"Some people say there is one doctor of the mind per civilian."

"Why do you think that is?"

"Because our home is crazy, and so we learn to become crazy to match it. Just as your home is beautiful, and you are beautiful to match it."

Toni chuckles. "Enough. You are the interesting one, sir. Not me."

He mimes opening the pages of a novel and says with a wicked gleam in his eye, "Open book, Toni. As advertised."

Shaking her head, she takes a tentative sip of her drink and finds that it isn't quite as revolting as it was the first time around. In fact, it's kind of grown on her. There's a sort of pleasing interplay between the mellow sweetness of the soda and the spicy bitterness of the liquor. And when she holds it up to the light, she sees that the drink isn't as ugly and brown as she thought originally. In fact, it turns a lovely emerald—but only if she gets the angle just right, like it's hiding that secret inner beauty from her.

"Whose turn is it now?" Nicolas asks.

"I don't know," Toni answers, "but all this back-and-forth is making my head spin. Let's do ten questions at a time, lighting-round style."

"Lightning round?" he says, confused.

She can't help but poke at him. "I thought you were Mr. World Traveler?" Then, taking pity, she adds, "It just means that we go fast."

He runs a hand over his chin thoughtfully. "You Americans are always trying to get things done quickly."

"Is that so?"

"Very much."

"I'll take your word for it. Now, get ready, because here we go." She leans forward, arms folded on the table in front of her, grinning playfully.

"*Dios mío.* Nothing hard, okay?"

"No promises. Let's start. What's your middle name?"

"Benjamin."

"Really? Who were you named after?"

"Benjamin Franklin, *claro.* The man who caught lightning in a bottle."

"You're joking."

"I would never."

Toni makes a mental note to circle back around on that hilarious tidbit. For now, though, she presses on. "What is your favorite color?"

"Pink. It reminds me of my daughter."

"Can you sing?"

"Not even to save my life."

"Why were you rude to me at the airport?"

"I thought you were drunk, to be honest."

Toni yelps, almost offended. "I had just gotten off a sixteen-hour flight!"

"Is that a question?"

"No, no, you're right. Umm...what's your earliest memory?"

"Sitting in my mother's lap while she knitted."

"Favorite season?"

"Summer."

"Favorite English word?"

"Serendipity."

She nods. "That's a good word. Last question: are you a good man, Nicolas?"

He must notice the shift in her voice because his face grows somber, and he leans in just a fraction closer. There is a long, pregnant pause before he parts his lips to speak.

"I think I am," he says carefully. "But do any of us ever know for sure?"

Toni considers for a second. "I think that's the kind of thing a good man would say," she decides.

He nods, and they each retreat to their drinks for a minute to chew over whatever the heck just happened between them. The bar patrons chatter on all sides, but in their flowery little bubble, it feels as though she and he are the only two people present.

Nicolas sets his drink down on the table again with a gentle clink. "You didn't ask me about my wife."

Toni's face flushes. "That's not my business."

"It's okay," Nicolas reassures her. "You could have. You should have."

"I just didn't want to...you know. Upset anyone."

"I see. Well, I should tell you that I lied."

She balks. "What? When?"

"Just now. You asked why I was rude to you at the airport. I lied. I was rude to you because my wife had just told me that she wanted a divorce. That is why I was rude."

"Oh." Toni falls back in her seat. "Oh," she says again, then feels dumb for repeating herself with such a nonsense reply. "I'm sorry."

"It is hardly your fault, *bella*."

"I can be sorry for things that aren't my fault, you know."

The corner of his mouth twitches up in a quick grin. "I suppose you can. But you don't need to waste your sympathy on me. It is as much my fault as it is hers."

"I see."

"We were separated for a long time. Young and in love are not lasting attributes unless you work to make them so. I learned that the hard way. So the relationship, it was dead already, long dead. But the divorce... it is difficult to see your failures written down on official letterhead, you know?"

"Yeah," Toni whispers. She glances down at her hands. "Yeah, I know what that's like."

"You said you had a husband, yes?"

"Once upon a time. That feels like lifetimes ago, though."

"These things always do."

"Did your love fade?"

"He was unfaithful."

"A fool, then."

"In more ways than one, yes."

Nicolas reaches out hesitantly and touches his hand to the back of hers, light as a feather. "Something I heard that helped me recently: we are not defined by what we have lost, Toni."

She looks at him and wonders how he can sequester so much in those eyes of his. There's fire and arrogance and sorrow swirling in there, all mixed together, and there's no telling which might boil to the surface at any given moment.

She looks down to her hands then, with Nicolas's callused fingertips resting on top, and surprises herself with what she says next. "I don't know about that. Sometimes I think that's all I'm defined by."

She feels a tear welling up at the corner of her eye and screams inwardly at herself to make it go away. He is going to think that she is an absolute lunatic. It's bizarre how she feels her gut being yanked in a million different directions all at once as if someone had secretly snagged her with dozens of fishhooks and started pulling her insides out.

Nicolas's hand rises from the table to lift her chin—gently, slowly—so that her eyes are forced to meet his. She lets him, for reasons she's not entirely sure of.

His eyes are alive, and his head is framed by the bouquet of flowers resting on the ledge behind him. He looks like a painting, too perfect for words. And when he speaks, he enunciates his words carefully, though they're still flecked with that beautiful silvery edge of his accent.

"I think that's the kind of thing a good woman would say, Toni."

The fishhooks in her ribs ease up. And for the first time since Henry died, she thinks to herself, *Maybe.*

Maybe there is more.

Maybe there is hope.

Maybe, maybe, maybe.

## 9

NANTUCKET, MASSACHUSETTS —JULY 2, 2000

Toni made a promise to herself as she boarded the plane the next morning: *no more tears.* The whole length of the flight to Nantucket, she repeated that oath in her head again and again until the words lost their meaning and got all mushed together into gibberish.

*No more tears. Nom ore tears. Nom ort ears.*

Gibberish or not, it got her through takeoff and landing. Toni didn't realize how hard she was working to keep that string of syllables at the forefront of her brain. At least, not until—almost simultaneously with the wheels of the plane hitting the ground—she felt a huge wave of exhaustion crash over her.

Now, the rest of her thoughts were running to gibberish, too, enough so that she accidentally stared at the flight attendant for far too long when the kindly older woman wished her a good day and asked if she'd enjoyed the flight.

"Are you all right, ma'am?" the uniformed woman asked, her eyebrows wrinkling in concern. When she reached out and laid a caring hand on Toni's elbow, Toni flinched.

Being touched right now felt like far too much to deal with. She felt like her whole body had turned into one exposed nerve ending. The merest brush of a stranger, no matter how well-meaning, sent frightened jitters coursing through her.

"Fine, thanks," she mumbled. She shouldered her bag and took off down the aisle in a hurry, head down and cheeks burning with—with what? Shame? Fear? The beginnings of a breakdown? She wasn't sure, and she didn't have any interest in delving further. Instead, she tried to stave it all off, whatever it was, until she had a glass or three of wine and a friendly shoulder to cry on.

For now, though, the mantra was the same: *nomoretears nomoretears nomoretears.*

She bustled into the terminal, keeping her head down as best as she could without bumping into the other folks disembarking. Toni had always thought that the Nantucket airport was far cuter than any airport had the right to be. It looked as if a charming gray house had sprouted antennas and an air traffic control station from its top floor.

If she looked out the window, she knew she'd be able to see row after row of little prop engine planes lined up like the toys in Brent's bedroom. They usually belonged to the rich folks who kept a second or third home up in Siasconset and liked to jet away to the island whenever they could take a break from their busy lives in the city. It never failed to astound her that such rickety, phony-looking contraptions could take to the sky like birds.

Beyond the planes was a bright blue sky, and not much else she could see from here. She'd forced herself not to look out the window of the plane as they'd approached the runway. She wanted her first look at Nantucket to come with all the sensations it deserved: toes in the sand, wine in the system, laughter on her lips. And if she had to fake that last one—well, then she was prepared to do just that.

Mae was waiting in the lobby for her when she rounded the corner. "Hi, Toni!" she exclaimed.

Walking up, Toni enveloped her in a hug. "It's so good to see you," she murmured into Mae's hair. "You smell nice."

"Oh thank you! Henry bought me a bottle of perfume as an apology after the whole cast iron pan debacle. I don't know who picked it out for him because the good Lord knows my husband doesn't know the first thing about women's perfume, but whoever it was, she did a good job. Almost made me forgive him for the pan." She winked.

Toni wanted to sag into Mae's arms and fall asleep then and there. There was something so beautifully simple and encouraging about Mae in that moment. To think of a life filled with petty bickering over silly household things that never truly mattered in the end, of sheepish apologies from a husband to his wife...the thought of a kiss and an "I'm sorry," of a dining table with smiling children's faces in every seat...it seemed like too much. Like Mae's home was Eden.

It wasn't Eden, of course. It was just Nantucket. But sometimes, the line between the two seemed wonderfully thin.

"How was your flight?" Mae asked. "Here, give me that." She reached down and plucked the bag from Toni's hands over her protests.

"Thanks," Toni sighed. Her neck had begun aching out of nowhere. She reached up a hand to rub out the kinks. "I'm falling apart, Mae."

"You and me both," her sister-in-law clucked, sounding not the least bit distressed about it. "I've got a bad knee that sounds like firecrackers shooting off every time I go up and down the stairs. The kids hear me coming from a mile away. I can't catch them up to any mischief these days."

Toni laughed. "Your kids? Mischievous? I'd have to see it to believe it."

"They've got you fooled ten ways to Sunday, darling. My younger two most especially."

"That's the Henry in them, right?"

Mae clicked her teeth. "I'd certainly hope so! I was a well-behaved little girl."

Toni threw a gentle, teasing elbow into Mae's ribs as they pushed through the doors and out into the warmth of the parking lot outdoors. "I'm sure you weren't all sunshine and roses."

Mae grinned, a flash of her own brand of mischief that looked just like Henry's. Two peas in a pod, her and him. It was still a marvel to Toni that there existed a pair of people in this world who were as perfect for each other as her brother and his wife. As always, she felt the twin pang of envy and the simple joy of seeing loved ones be happy. She tried to ignore how much more the envy stung today than it normally did.

"Well, there was this one time..."

"Mhmm. That's what I thought."

Mae hefted Toni's luggage into the trunk and closed it. With the time creeping close to noon, the sun was almost directly overhead. It shone down bright and beautiful. The sky stretched in an unbroken field of cerulean blue from horizon to horizon. Toni closed her eyes and indulged in a brief, bizarre daydream about grabbing hold of a balloon and letting it carry her off into that never-ending blueness. Blue above, blue below, bluer and bluer everywhere she looked...

"Toni?" Mae asked. "You ready to go? You look a little tired, dear."

"Yes," Toni said with a smile. "I'm ready."

They both clambered into the car. Mae pulled out carefully after checking and double-checking for oncoming traffic—she had always been a bit of a nervous driver. "I've got your room made up for you already. Holly and Eliza are bunking together, which has thrilled both of them, I assure you."

"You didn't have to do that to the girls," Toni said with guilt.

"Nonsense. They'll be just fine. Teenage girls are a hardy lot, if a bit whiny when the mood strikes."

"Truer words were never spoken."

They wound their way out of the airport and picked up Old South Road. Toni drank in the sights as they passed outside of her window: Nantucket Gray and Gardener Green paint on all the houses, weathered siding and shingled roofs basking in the noontime glow, split-rail fences wrought with Virginia creepers and greenbriers fighting for light.

Old South Road took them to the turnaround right at the rim of downtown. They swung left and followed the edge of the main drag, past the bank and the Stop & Shop. Then they continued away from the hubbub, towards where the houses spread apart once more and the sense of salty calm thickened in the air.

Just before they left the last of the shops behind them, Toni noticed something and frowned. "That lot hasn't always been empty, has it?" She pointed towards a barren patch of grass and dirt off to the right.

They were paused to let a cute little blonde family cross the street, Mom and Dad each holding one of their child's hands. Mae looked to where Toni was pointing.

"No, it hasn't. That used to be...now, what was it? I can't recall. Sometimes I think my brain is getting as bad as my knee."

"The B&B."

"Of course, that's right." Mae slapped Toni on the thigh. "You were always the brighter Benson, isn't that so?" She stage-winked, which would've normally gotten a small chuckle out of Toni.

But Toni was too busy gazing wistfully at the spot where the bed and breakfast used to be. "That was the one that Patricia and Marcus owned, right? The Partridges?"

"Mhmm, yep, that's exactly it."

"What happened?"

The Partridges had been friends with Toni and Henry's parents for a long time. They'd owned and operated a small six-room homestay there. Their guests raved about how delightful the place was, and they had regulars come back year after year after year. It seemed odd for them to just close up shop when they'd been doing quite well as far as Toni was aware.

"I believe their granddaughter got quite sick, poor thing, so they sold the place and moved to Philadelphia to help care for her with their son and his wife."

"What a shame. I'm sorry to hear about their granddaughter."

"Yes, very sad. They were a nice couple."

Toni couldn't help but frown. There was something jarring about coming back to the place where you grew up and realizing that the reality of it doesn't match your memories anymore. She felt unsettled, almost nauseous, and she decided that she'd better go down for a nap once she got back to Mae's house.

"I told you Henry would be gone for the weekend, right?" Mae said suddenly, as if she'd just remembered.

"You told me, yes. Guy thinks he's slick, getting out of Dodge just when his sister arrives."

"He certainly does. But you know what it's like trying to keep him cooped up when he's yearning to hit the water."

Toni chuckles. "I shudder to think of it. I certainly don't envy you the challenge, that's for sure."

"I wasn't going to stand in his way, believe you that. Better with him out of our hair anyway, don't you think?" They pulled into the driveway. "Well, here we are! Home sweet home." Mae put the car in park and looked over at Toni. "The kids are all out, for a change, so we're in luck. I believe Lola tempted them down the street with a batch of brownies. But I imagine maybe you'd like to just go lie down for a while before you face that particular hurricane anyway, hm?"

"I think that's probably a good suggestion."

"Let's do that then, dear. Come, I'll help you get settled in, and then I'll let you rest for a while before dinner. I've got a glass of wine with your name on it when the time comes."

"You keep the glass; give me the bottle..." Toni had meant it as a joke, but it came out a bit more bitter than she intended.

Mae smiled politely, but tilted her head and looked over to where Toni sat in the passenger seat. She'd clearly heard a note in Toni's voice that sounded a touch wrong. "Is everything okay, hon?" she asked. She said it in such a way—such a Mae way—that Toni came closer than she had yet to the complete breakdown that was waiting for its chance to come upon her. Perilously close, so close she could already feel the tears welling up behind her eyes and threatening to erupt.

She closed her eyes for a second and said her mantra silently —*nomoretears.* Then she opened them again and coaxed her lips into a reasonable facsimile of a smile.

"I've just had a long day of travel," she said. "I'll be right as rain by dinnertime."

Mae waited for one long moment to see if Toni would offer up any other tells before she nodded and turned off the ignition. "Of course," she smiled. "I'd expect nothing less of you."

The two women got out of the car, retrieved Toni's bag from the trunk, and made their way inside. It smelled like vanilla and rose candles in the house, which Toni knew was because Mae had somewhat of an addiction to a particular brand of them, handcrafted by a local artisan. It was a warm, welcoming smell, and she took the chance to pause in the entryway and relish in it.

Toni gently plucked her luggage out of Mae's grasp. "Upstairs, second door on the left, right?"

"You got it," Mae said with another trademark wink. "I'll make sure the kids are quiet when they come home. First one to utter a peep is getting sold for parts."

Toni laughed as she turned and mounted the stairs while Mae went into the kitchen. She heard the burner click on, but when she slipped into her bedroom for the weekend and closed the door, that sound faded away. All that was left was the distant ocean roar and the comfortable sighs of an old house settling deeper and deeper into its foundation.

She set her bag down by the bureau, took off her shoes, and laid down. She knew she ought to change clothes, air travel being somewhat of a haven for germs. But she was so tired suddenly that she could barely keep her eyes open.

"Just thirty seconds," she said out loud to the empty room. "Then I'll get up and change for my nap."

She was out before her head hit the pillow.

~

Toni woke up to someone's face filling her entire field of vision.

She had to stifle a terrified shriek before she realized that it was just her nephew Brent, who'd clambered onto the bed and was trying to touch his nose to hers.

"Brent, honey! You scared the daylights out of me," she said.

Mae came rushing in a moment later, brandishing a wooden spoon like a battle ax. "Brent Evan Benson!" she yelled. "What did I tell you about letting Aunt Toni sleep?"

He started to stammer something and looked like he was on the verge of tears. Toni interceded. "It's okay," she said. She swept the four-year-old up into her arms and planted a kiss on top of his blond head. "Aunt Toni had a good nap, and she wanted to see you anyway."

"I'm sorry, Toni," Mae said. She sighed and let the spoon fall by her side. Everyone in the house knew that Mae didn't have the heart to ever actually use the thing, but that didn't stop her from charging into the middle of Benson child mayhem like an armed Viking if the furor ever got too loud.

"No, no, really, it's okay. I oughta be getting up anyhow. What time is it?"

"Just shy of five o'clock," Mae said. She turned to leave the room before stopping to add, "Oh, I invited Lola and Debra over for dinner as well! I hope you don't mind?"

"Of course not!" Toni said. "It'll be good to see those old hens."

Mae laughed. "Make sure you say that to their faces," she said. "They'll have some choice words to say back, I'm sure. I've gotta go check on the lobster. Do you mind?"

"Go do your thing, hon. Can I help with anything?"

"Not a chance!"

"Aunt Toni," Brent said cheerily once his mother had retreated back downstairs, "can we read a book?"

Toni grinned. "Nothing in the whole wide world would make me happier. Why don't you go pick one out, and I'll meet you on the porch? We can sit in the rocking chair and read together. How's that sound?"

Brent *wheeee*'d his way out of the room in a blaze, leaving Toni chuckling in his wake. She groaned and kept working out the kinks in her neck as she sat upright. The airplane seat really had done a number on her muscles, though it had helped somewhat to nap for as long as she did.

She changed quickly into a pair of comfortable jeans and a white cotton T-shirt. Then she padded downstairs.

The lower floor was rich with the aroma of butter and stock. Toni was sorely tempted to go peek into the kitchen to see what Mae was whipping up, but Brent was waiting by the front door already, book in hand and shifting excitedly from foot to foot. He looked like he might erupt if she denied him their promised book time for even a second longer.

So she went over to him, opened the door, and they went out onto the porch. "Up you come!" she cooed as she hefted the boy into her lap. "Let's see what we have here—oo, *The Hungry Hungry Caterpillar*. Good choice."

They cracked open the book together and started to read. Brent insisted on turning the pages and calling out the names of all the animals he recognized in the illustrations, so it took them a while to get through it. But Toni didn't mind. She had her nephew on her lap, a house brimming with good food around her, and in the distance, the Nantucket summer sun looked like it was veering closer and closer towards retiring for the day.

Soon enough, two familiar figures came wheeling their bikes up the driveway. "Look who it is!" Toni whispered in Brent's ear. "Why don't you go surprise Miss Lola and Miss Debra with big hugs?"

Brent, ever willing to be involved in a secret scheme, agreed with a fervent nod. He popped down from Toni's lap and went racing off towards the two women.

"Hi, Toni!" they called out once Brent's hugs had been received and he'd run off, distracted by a soccer ball left in the front yard. They stepped onto the porch and gave her each a kiss on the cheek.

"In town for the Fourth?" Lola asked.

"Mhmm," confirmed Toni.

"Did you manage to get rid of your husband, too? Or is he lurking within?"

Debra was only joking, but Toni winced anyway. She pretended to reach up a hand and rub at her neck, hoping that it would serve as sufficient distraction to play off the sudden pang in her heart at the reminder of Jared. She'd actually managed to go a few hours without thinking of him, miracle of miracles. But Debra's jest had brought him right back to the forefront of her mind.

"Something like that," she said lamely. "Mae's inside. Should we go in?"

Lola and Debra nodded. It didn't seem like they'd noticed anything out of the ordinary, for which Toni was grateful. She called out to Brent, who joined them as they all went back into the house.

A little while later, they were all seated in the dining room and ready to eat. The table was practically groaning with the ungodly amount of food Mae had prepared.

"My goodness," Lola exclaimed, "did you think you were feeding an army?"

"Just you wait," Mae replied knowingly. "These children look innocent, but they're a pack of hyenas when it comes to dinnertime."

Eliza rolled her eyes, and Holly and Sara followed suit immediately.

"You girls look gorgeous," Toni said quietly. "You're all growing up so fast."

She knew that it was a bit of a cheesy thing to say, and certainly not the kind of thing that sixteen-, thirteen-, or eleven-year-old girls could care about hearing from their aunt. But she just couldn't help herself.

Mae said a quick grace before pointing out the dishes to identify them. "We've got lobster chowder and baked cod, both of which Mr. Dave from the fish shop caught himself this morning. The scallops, too. Corn on the cob and coleslaw, as well as pasta salad—I made a side dish for you with no tomatoes, Sara—and string beans. Toni, ladies, please help yourselves to as much wine as you can possibly drink. And you, Mr. Brent, young sir, had better finish all of your chicken nuggets if you want to have any chance of getting some of the rum raisin ice cream that Miss Debra was kind enough to bring. Is that all? I think that's all. Let's eat!"

They dug in gratefully. Everybody except for Toni that is. As everyone else around the table began ladling out chowder and vegetables onto their dishes, she sat back for a moment with an irrepressible smile on her face.

It was a beautiful sight to see, to feel, to partake in. This was a happy house, and even if Henry's absence was noted, it still felt so bursting at the seams with pure joy that it was impossible not to grin from ear to ear.

So what if she was running from sorrow she never expected or asked for? So what if her heart throbbed painfully whenever the merest thought of Jared crossed her mind (and almost all of her thoughts led to Jared, one way or another, just as all roads lead to Rome)?

So what, so what, so what?

She *had* to be happy here, and she was grateful that the choice between happiness and misery had been taken right out of her hands because there was no telling which way she might lean if she'd had to pick between the two on her own.

She *had* to be happy here. After all, this was home.

# 10

Toni feels like she has been sleepwalking for the last seven days.

After their date, Nicolas walked her back to her hotel. He stopped outside of the door to face her. She watched him with bated breath, feeling like she was on the precipice of something foreign and terrifying and exciting all at once. It was how she imagined skydiving would be—knowing that she was about to jump out of a perfectly good plane, one that had gotten her this far problem-free, and questioning whether she was stark-raving mad for considering the leap at all.

She wondered if he was going to try to kiss her. She wondered also if she would let him.

In the end, it didn't matter, because he didn't try. He merely squeezed her hand, nodded once—crisply, as if they were settling a business transaction—and took off into the night.

She caught just a glimpse of his eyes before he was gone. They were stormy with emotions she could not and still cannot decipher, no matter how many times she's thought of them in the days and nights since.

The odd departure has left her unsettled. She knows this makes no sense at all, but it feels as if the entire country changed shape when she wasn't looking. The buildings, the people, the food—they look different, sound different, taste different. She can't put her finger on *what* exactly has changed; all she knows is that something has very definitely shifted beneath her feet.

The things that have been bringing her pleasure in the two months of this experience—reading books in cafés, strolling through the city's many parks—now make her irritable and impatient. And things that she would've walked right past not so long ago now captivate her completely. She darn near cried the other day when she caught sight of a rainbow refracted in an oil slick on an empty cobblestone side street in Palermo. It seemed like such a fragile and temporary beauty. If she didn't stop and look at it, who would?

She knows of course that all these things point back to Nicolas, even if she refuses to acknowledge that during her waking hours. That date was the moment everything changed. Not just the date—the moment when his fingers lifted her chin, and he looked into her eyes and told her that she wasn't defined by what she had lost.

That was a ridiculous thing to say. She is *exclusively* defined by what she has lost. Aren't we all? How can anyone say otherwise?

She does her best not to dwell on thoughts like that, though. They aren't leading anywhere productive, and they certainly aren't doing anything to help dispel the sorrow that Henry's passing still burdens her with.

So she has just stuck to her routine, stubbornly, even when it seems as if all the pleasure has been wrung out of it like a wet towel. She drinks coffee that tastes flavorless, she reads the same page of the same book again and again (because she forgets what she's just read as soon as she finishes reading it), she takes walks that leave her more anxious than she was before she began them.

And she wonders where the world will bring her next.

She hears a knock on her door. She's been holding a book open for close to half an hour now, and she hasn't yet turned a page. It isn't hard to put it down and go see who might be calling upon her.

"Cami!" she says when she opens the door and sees her friend standing there. "Looking chic as always."

That's not a lie—Cami is dressed to the nines, which is no surprise to anyone who's spent any amount of time with the woman. Today's ensemble is a long black shirt-dress, sheer in sections, with black fishnet tights, a massive aquamarine-colored scarf, and bright yellow ballet flats. Otherworldly, gorgeous, and totally Camille.

"Would you expect anything else from me, love?" she says with a lascivious wink.

"Well, go on, then, give us a show," Toni teases.

Camille obliges, twirling in the hallway as both women laugh.

"Only you," muses Toni. "Only you can put an outfit like that together and make it work."

"Yes, well, I'd have preferred to be blessed with a large endowment, but we don't get to pick our gifts, now, do we?"

"I suppose not. Come in, come in. My humble abode awaits you."

Camille whisks in, leaving a trail of deliciously subtle perfume in her wake. "I like what you've done with the place," she jokes.

Honestly, living in a hotel hasn't been too bad at all. Certainly not as bad as Toni thought it would be. Perhaps it's just that it's nice to be on the receiving end of top-notch service after years of being the one doing the serving at her inn. Waiting on strangers hand and foot gets awfully tiring after a while. This is a good change of pace.

Besides, she spends most of her time outside, even on the days when the clouds crowd low and gray over the buildings, and the winds whistling down the streets are a bit icy. That doesn't overly bother her. *A good coat solves more problems than you might expect*—something her mother said more times than Toni can possibly count. As with most of Angeline Benson's expressions, it holds a great deal of truth.

"What brings you to my neck of the woods today?" Toni asks. "Can I get you anything? Coffee, tea...?"

"Nothing for me, thanks," Camille says as she sets aside the book Toni had been reading and settles down into the unoccupied armchair. "I came to invite you to a party, of course! What good is a local friend if I don't bring you around town?"

"Oh, erm," Toni hedges as she walks around the room, straightening things that don't really need straightening. "I don't know if I'm in much of a partying mood, I'm afraid."

"Nonsense," scolds Camille at once in that nonchalant way of hers. "One glass of good wine will rinse that hesitation right out of you. Besides," she adds with a mischievous gleam in her eye, "I have a suggestion."

"Uh-oh. Now you've truly got me concerned."

"A plus-one could be—how do you say, eh... just the ticket, don't you think?"

"No. Cami, no, no, no. I don't—"

"Toni, women our age simply don't have the luxury of playing coy. I learned a long time ago that the world is far simpler when you just admit what you want, then reach out and take it. It's a truth that men are taught and women are shielded from, in my experience. Quite a shame. Women are much better at it."

Toni hides behind her laughter for a second as she weighs what Camille is saying.

She's been hesitant to reach out to Nicolas again after their date. He texted her the following day—just a simple, *I had an enjoyable evening with you. I stand by what I said: you are a very interesting woman*—but Toni didn't respond.

That was dumb, she knows. She ought to respond. She ought to do exactly what Camille is suggesting.

Nicolas intrigues her. He is handsome and interesting and courteous, and now that they have uncovered the source of his rudeness during their first encounter, all of her inexplicable irritation towards him has vanished. In fact, she feels closer to him, knowing that he has looked down at divorce papers just like she did and wondered where it all went wrong.

It isn't a stretch to say that she actually likes him now. He certainly seems to like her, doesn't he? The question is, what does that *mean*? Or rather, what should it mean? What could it mean? What might it mean if she gives it the chance to develop?

She isn't anywhere close to answering those kinds of questions.

"I sense a little unease," Camille comments wryly. "And yet, I am choosing to ignore it. Blame my Frenchness. Give me your phone, then, if you're going to be so hand-wringy about it."

Toni isn't sure if it's the right decision, but in the end, it's much easier to give in to a strong personality like Camille's than to keep going round and round in circles with her. She retrieves her phone from the nightstand and hands it over to her friend. She feels both guilty and excited at the same time as Camille pecks out a text message. Then she hears the *whoosh* noise of a text making its way out into the world, and she knows that there's no point in being anxious anymore; the damage is done.

"That's that, then, isn't it?"

Camille nods. "Yes, it is."

"What'd you say?"

"I asked for his hand in marriage."

Toni promptly chucks a pillow at her friend's head, and then sinks into the armchair next to her, both of them chuckling.

*It feels like having a sister,* Toni thinks to herself. She is then immediately buried in a tsunami of guilt at the thought of Henry. Is this what moving on feels like? Because it seems awfully close to forgetting, and that is as unforgivable a sin as she can dream up. But where is the line between the two? She doesn't know. She just does not know.

"I'm only kidding, just so you know," Camille adds to clarify. "I just said we were headed to a little gathering tonight and asked if he'd like to join. Anyway, I've got to do a few things around town. Would you like to join me, or should I just swing by and scoop you up this evening?"

"Go ahead without me," Toni says. "I'll just see you tonight."

Camille nods and rises. "Sounds good, *cariño.* I'll see you tonight."

~

That night, an hour or so after the sun has descended behind the buildings and the first blush of night purple is smearing across the sky, Toni finds herself hustling along a busy sidewalk, arm in arm with Camille.

Camille spies him before Toni does. "Adventure sighted," she whispers mischievously.

Toni looks up to see what her friend is talking about. She sees him, too: a familiar figure standing on the corner ahead. The crowd of pedestrians parts around Nicolas like a school of fish avoiding a shark, giving him a wide berth on all sides.

"Hi," Toni says sheepishly when they step up to him.

Nicolas smiles. "Good evening, Toni," he sees. He stoops down to their height and grazes his cheek against each of the women's, the way Argentines say hello to each other. Camille relinquishes Toni's elbow, leaving her feeling stranded between the two of them and uncertain which way to lean.

A gust of wind blows, this one with fangs. Toni shivers. "It's cold tonight," she mumbles.

"Let's go inside then, shall we?" Camille suggests. She glances up at Nicolas, who nods and gestures for her to lead the way.

Camille sets off striding down the block, a stretch of nice apartments recently painted with a coat of white that gleams against the worn sidewalks. Toni hesitates for just a second before she falls in step with Nicolas, and the two of them form the base of a triangle with Camille at the head.

Without saying a word, Nicolas takes Toni's hand in hers. She looks down at it in surprise, then up at him.

Then she smiles and says nothing, just grips his fingers back in her own.

Grateful for the warmth. Grateful for the touch. Grateful for how normal and simple and beautiful it feels to hold hands with someone and not make much of a fuss about it whatsoever.

Camille leads them into an apartment building. The three of them bundle into an elevator, which soon deposits them onto a floor of apartment units. One of the doors is open. Light, warmth, and music spill out of it, along with the delicious tang of chimichurri and the sizzle of steaks on the grill.

Their arrival is greeted with a boisterous roar of laughter and hellos. Camille brings Nicolas and Toni on a whirlwind tour of the room. There are hands to shake and cheeks to kiss, wines to sample and cheeses to nibble on. Toni knows she can't possibly remember who is who, so she does her best to just smile and nod. It doesn't seem to matter—each person in the room is as friendly as the next.

As they whisk around, Toni is struck by the feeling of how this all just fits together: good food, kind friends, a warm eddy of people all tucked in together so that the cold seeping in through the cracked-open windows doesn't seem so foreboding anymore. Laughter and wine belong hand in hand, the way she and Nicolas are. He hasn't let go of her for more than a moment since they entered, even when he is shaking hands and kissing cheeks of his own.

Toni watches him as he talks, switching back and forth effortlessly between Spanish and English. He seems supremely comfortable, though he doesn't know any more people here than she does (which is to say, zero).

She likes watching him converse. There is just something ineffably elegant about the way he modulates his pride with warmth, like he can choose to turn the faucet of his charisma on and off as he pleases. She's content to stay nestled against his side, wineglass in hand, and listen to him chatter.

The evening swirls to and fro. People migrate from the living room to the terrace to the dinner table. Food is eaten, and bottle after bottle of wine goes down with ease. The laughter never ceases.

Toni, never having been much of a partier, is happy to watch it all from the heart of things. She answers questions when people ask them of her, and she tells stories about Nantucket, about her family, about running the inn if Nicolas coaxes her into them.

Mostly, though, she just listens and basks in the kind of good-times familiarity she didn't realize she needed quite so badly.

The hours melt together like the creamy mushroom-and-quinoa risotto that Toni eats perhaps a bit too much of. It's almost a shame when the time comes for folks to begin trickling out, headed for home.

One by one, as people leave—all of them stopping to joke with her and kiss her on the cheek on their way out—she feels a piece of the warmth leave the room with them, like when someone you're cuddling with in bed begins slowly to roll away from you.

Soon, Camille comes up to them. "Ready to go, *cariños*?" she asks of Toni and Nicolas.

Nicolas looks down at Toni and arches an eyebrow. "Are you?"

She glances at her watch and is surprised to see that it's close to two in the morning. She hasn't yawned even once, which is highly unusual for her, being more of a morning person than a night owl.

She shrugs. "That's probably for the best. I'm an old lady. I think it's against the rules to watch the sun come up if I haven't slept a wink."

Camille rolls her eyes, though she's merely teasing. She's close to Toni's age, but she never makes jokes about growing older. *"I am as young as I choose to be"* is a Camille-ism that Toni has heard more than once. "As you wish. Let me just say goodbye to everyone."

They all take their own turns winding through the crowd and thanking the hosts and new friends. Then they, too, tug on their coats and scarves and slip back out into the night.

"Did you have fun?" Camille asks of Toni as they stride down the sidewalk. The night air around them is cool and crisp.

"Yes," Toni replies with a smile. "Your friends are very nice. And the food was to die for."

"And you, Nicolas?" Camille inquires, turning her face up to the man, who has a protective arm draped carelessly around Toni.

"It was an enjoyable evening, yes," he says simply. His cheeks are slightly flushed with wine. Toni can't help but notice how handsome he looks under the streetlights. They illuminate the sharp cut of his jaw and the pallor of his eyes. She clings to his coat, grateful for the warmth his bulk provides.

"Good. I'm glad. Well, this is me," she says. She stops at a corner and points down a side street towards where her apartment is. *"Buenas noches, cariños,"* Camille says. Toni gives her friend a kiss on the cheek. Nicolas does the same.

Then, with one more farewell wave, Camille slinks away. Toni and Nicolas stand still for a moment and watch her go until she's swallowed up by the shadows.

"Well?" Nicolas asks when she's gone. "Which way are you?"

Toni points straight ahead. "Just a little farther that way. Five or six blocks."

"Lead the way," he says, gesturing. She smiles and pulls closer under his arm. He smells good—the lingering scent of the food still clinging to his clothes, along with that alluring mix of cologne and man musk that she always notices on him.

It feels right to say nothing, to let the simple fact of contact between them do all the conversing. They walk slowly, in no hurry to be anywhere in particular.

A few folks rush past—other drunken couples ambling unsteadily from the bars, families with sleeping children in their arms, club kids just now heading out to the massive, bass-pounding nightclubs dotted around the city.

They cross the street, turn around the corner of a building, and see a throng of people gathered in a big alcove set against the side of the concrete structure.

As they get closer, Toni begins to hear something: music, the familiar aching moan of a tango that has yet to hit its full stride.

"Do you want to take a peek?" Nicolas asks. She glances up and sees that he's smiling at her with an amused look on his face.

She blushes. "Was I that obvious?"

"Open book," he teases.

She rolls her eyes and bites back a smile as they meander over to the gathered pedestrians. When they've joined the circle, she finds a window of space between two folks on the inner ring and looks in.

There is a couple in the cleared space at the center of the circle. One is a man in full, formal tango gear—a black waistcoat, black button-down shirt, and the full-legged black pants that performers wear. His shiny black leather shoes have a prominent heel that clacks on the cobblestones with every stride.

His partner is in a provocative scarlet dress that shimmers each time she turns and whirls. She is fit and beautiful, and Toni gasps aloud as she pirouettes rapidly and collapses towards the ground gracefully, saved only at the last minute by her partner's strong arm from cracking her head against the ground. Her shoes, in a scarlet that matches the color of her dress, are alight with sequins.

The source of their music is just a speaker set against the wall behind them, but the music crackling out of it does the job well enough. Toni watches, mesmerized, as the song crescendos, and the couple responds with their longest and fastest steps yet.

The woman's body is long and lithe, and her partner has an effortless sense of balance that makes him seem like the sun at the center of the universe as this gorgeous, feminine comet careens around him. They mingle, then separate, never fully losing touch, but going just far enough and fast enough apart that Toni gasps again and again, sure that this is the moment when they will lose control.

But she is wrong each time. They are dancing right on the edge of chaotic, and she thinks to herself that perhaps that is where the beauty comes from: from leaning all the way into the drama and the passion of it all, close enough to truly risk it.

Eventually, the song settles into its denouement. The dancers end pinned chest to chest, gazing into each other's eyes with smoldering heat. And when the last note fades, the audience bursts into applause.

The couple takes a bow, hand in hand, and then he sets a hat on the sidewalk for donations. Nearly everyone in the crowd drops a few bills into the receptacle before branching off into the night.

Toni waits until there is space for her to step forward and leave a bit of her appreciation behind for the performers.

She feels a sudden coolness and glances up to see that Nicolas has strode over to the dancers. They converse quickly, a bill changes hands, and then Nicolas turns to her and smiles. As he does, Toni notices the woman behind him reach down to the speaker and start another song.

She assumes that the performers are going to go again at Nicolas's request. But they seem content to stay leaning against the building wall and smoking cigarettes while smiling at Toni.

She doesn't get what's happening until Nicolas steps up and puts his hand on the middle of her back in the classic tango position. Automatically, she responds by finding her own placement in his embrace.

"Dance with me," he murmurs in her ear.

"Here?" she yelps. She looks around to see a few passersby giving them curious glances, wondering if they are about to perform like the other buskers did.

"Anywhere you'll have me," is Nicolas's immediate, husky reply. It makes the hair on the back of her neck stand on end.

"You like being unpredictable, don't you?"

"You coax it out of me."

"Oh, so it's my fault?"

"Not your fault. But perhaps your problem." He winks. "Now, are we going to let the song pass us by, or will we dance?"

Toni looks up into his face. Those gray eyes are flashing like fish scales catching the moonlight. His smile—teasing and serious, cocky and humble all at once—is irresistible.

"One song," she says. "Then I'm going right to sleep. *Claro?*"

He laughs at her yeehaw-Yankee Spanish, but that's all the answer he gives before he finds the beat and pulls her into their first step.

She lets him lead, following closely, never wanting to be too far from him. It's easy to slip into the rhythm, to let the music and the man transport her away.

Not away from here, though. On the contrary, it transports her away from everywhere else she is that is *not here.*

It takes her away from Atlanta, from Jared, from Nantucket, from Henry.

It takes her away from guilt and shame, from regret and longing.

It takes her fully and completely into this moment. All of her is here, with Nicolas, with this song and this city and this night. Every molecule of Toni Benson is present and accounted for. Fully alive. Fully glistening with the force of her presence.

She feels like she is glowing from within.

The song ends, though Toni feels like it lasted hardly a heartbeat. As he always does, Nicolas clings to her once the last note fades, not yet ready to let her go.

He gazes down at her, unblinking.

"You are defined by far more than what you have lost, Toni," he whispers. He says it with the voice of a prophecy. "You are defined by whatever you choose to be defined by. I think it is best that we choose to be defined by what we love."

What on earth should she say to that? What *can* she say? It feels like he's casting a spell on her. Like this is the exact combination of words and sights and sounds and smells that she's needed for so long, in order to ease something in her that had begun to ache so badly for want of release.

She looks up at him. Her lips part as if she's going to speak, but when she tries, she comes up blank. She just doesn't have the words to say what that means to her. To tell Nicolas how abruptly he has become the center of her universe. She can't say that to him for many reasons, not the least of which is because he will surely think it is an insane thing to say to someone that you barely know.

"I...I..." she starts and stops and starts and stops again.

"It's okay," he says. "You don't have to tell me anything if you don't want to. I..." Now, it seems like it's Nicolas's turn to pause and search for the right words. He settles on saying, "I like you very much, Toni."

"I like you, too, Nicolas," she whispers, throat hoarse from the cold.

Then it happens, the moment she feared and longed for and did her best to ignore since the second she first sensed that the two of them were headed hurtling towards each other like shooting stars in the night sky.

He leans down the last little bit of the way and presses his lips gently to hers.

Nicolas's hand is still strong on her back as Toni kisses him in return. He tastes like red wine and the faint suggestion of a cigar. His stubble grazes delicately against her cheek.

The kiss doesn't last long. He pulls a half inch away from her and smiles again. "I like you very much," he repeats.

He lets his hand fall away from her back. Toni smiles and twines her fingers through his. "Walk me home," she says.

This time, she isn't letting him slip away from her and vanish into the darkness. She holds his hand as, together, they leave the performers behind them and head off into what is left of the night.

# 11

In the way that folks tend to do after massive family dinners, everyone sort of dispersed once the food was gone.

Brent was the first to go, racing after a firefly he saw flitting around on the other side of the window. Holly was dispatched to keep watch over him and make sure he didn't do anything overly foolish in the front yard.

Eliza mumbled an excuse and went to commandeer the landline so she could talk to a friend. Sara wasn't far behind her older sister, saying something about "catching up on her summer reading for school" that anyone with half a brain knew was a bald-faced lie.

The four women left behind finished the last of the second bottle of chardonnay, then spent the next twenty minutes happily scrubbing away at dishes, ignoring Mae's protests all the while.

"Hush, Mae," Debra scolded more than once. "We're happy to help if you would just let us."

Eventually, Mae conceded that it was a losing battle, and so little by little, the kitchen was cleansed of crumbs and stains. The leftover food

—of which there was plenty—was wrapped in tinfoil and stowed in the fridge, and a comfortable evening time quiet settled over the house.

When wash-up duty was done, the women all retired to the front yard to relieve Holly of her caretaker responsibilities. Toni was perfectly content to watch Brent continuing to chase the fireflies as if he had boundless energy—which, of course, he did. They chitchatted among themselves about life on the island, the comings and goings of the residents.

"You know," Mae said to Toni, "your old friend Kendra Adkins just had a baby a couple weeks ago."

"Is that so?" Toni said in surprise. "God, I haven't talked to her in so long. We were so close back in the day. Maybe I'll drop in on her tomorrow and check out the little one."

"Well," Debra said as she rose to her feet with a groan, "if you need me tomorrow, you can find me running laps around the island, trying to work off the fifty pounds I just gained."

"I'll join you, gladly," Lola chimed in. "I know I said I could eat my weight in lobster when we sat down, but I didn't realize it would come to pass quite so literally. You always get me, Mae."

"It's my pleasure every time, darling," Mae chuckled. Everyone hugged everyone, and then Lola and Debra ambled off down the lane, headed towards their houses a couple blocks up the road.

Mae and Toni sat quietly for a while in the rocking chairs. Brent was finally starting to slow down.

"I suppose I ought to bathe him eventually," Mae said, as much to herself as to Toni.

"Should I get the hose?" Toni joked.

"Don't tempt me." Mae smiled and drained the last of the bedtime tea she'd prepared for herself in lieu of a nightcap. "Ah well, can't stave off the inevitable. Are you going to stay out here, love?"

"Yeah," Toni nodded, "just for a bit. It's a nice night. I think I'll just soak it in for a while. I missed home."

"You got it. Can I bring you anything?"

"No, no, please. You've done more than enough. I'll be out here if you need me, or if Brent tries to make a naked run for it through the front door."

"You joke," Mae said wryly, "but it certainly wouldn't be the first time."

Laughing, she turned and called for Brent, who came barreling inside at full speed and right up the stairs. The boy did love his baths.

When the front door closed behind Mae, Toni was left with nothing but the crackle of ocean waves and the buzzing of fireflies to listen to, along with the occasional thump and splash from upstairs as Mae wrangled Brent into a state of semicleanliness.

Toni sighed. That felt good, like letting off some pent-up pressure, so she did it again.

What a night it had a been. What a day, what a week, what a life. She didn't know it was possible for someone to go through so many emotions in such a short period of time. "Roller coaster" didn't even begin to cover it. She'd aged twenty years in two days, it felt like, and the ride looked as if it had a long way to go yet.

When would it end? And when it did end, where would it leave her? She wasn't sure of that—wasn't sure of anything anymore, as a matter of fact. All the things she once took for granted were gone. She had no more husband, no more house. She supposed she still had a job, although the thought of stepping foot in that office ever again suddenly made her sick.

It wasn't fair of Jared to take that from her. She liked her house! She liked her job! She liked the life she had! And at the beginning of this week, it seemed like those things were in her life to stay.

But now, there was just this big, intimidating emptiness where her future once was, as formless and deep as the night sky stretching out over Nantucket. She didn't have the faintest idea how she was going to fill it.

She'd felt good at dinner. A sense of warm belonging had settled in, and the wine had sanded down the edges of her burgeoning grief.

Now, though, as she sat quietly with nothing but her thoughts for company, that warmth had begun to dissipate.

She shivered, even though the air itself was thick with summer humidity. It wasn't a temperature shiver—it was a shiver of the soul as it tried to find a comfortable place to rest its haunches.

But there was no comfort to be found. Maybe there wouldn't be comfort ever again.

Her thoughts went around and around like that, like a carousel whipping ever faster in its circle, and with every rotation, her sadness felt closer and denser, until she was nearly choking on it.

And then, when it had no more room inside of her chest to keep blooming, it came out of her, in the form of big, fat tears that she couldn't hold back no matter how hard she tried.

Maybe she needed another cry. But she sure as heck didn't want it. Crying was for babies, right? Didn't her mom teach her not to cry? That she had to hold her chin up if she wanted to play with the boys? *You can't let them get to you, Antonia,* her mother had said more than once. *You need to show them that you're every bit as strong as they are.*

Toni knew she was a strong woman. Her mother had been strong, right up to the end, and that same blood ran in her veins.

But the world just felt so heavy right now. It was too much for one woman to bear without at least crying a little bit.

So she let herself cry, and she pretended as though that was a conscious choice, even when she knew deep down in her bones that she was actually powerless to stop it.

"Toni?"

Toni glanced up and saw Mae standing on the threshold of the front door. She was framed by the light coming from within, and, coupled with the tears clouding Toni's eyes, it looked like she had a halo encircling her head. That was ridiculous—Mae was a good person, sure, as close to a saint as anyone that Toni knew. But she had her foibles just like the rest of us. Angelic, yes, but not an angel. Still, in that moment, it was hard to feel like Mae was anything but heaven-sent. As her sister-in-law swept over, sat down on the arm of the rocking chair, and pulled Toni into a tight hug, saying, "It's okay, darling, you cry all you need to," Mae looked angelic through and through.

Toni smelled Mae's perfume and the scent of the dinner they'd just eaten, and her skin was fresh and soapy from Brent's bath. She was warm and soft to the touch.

Toni needed all those things right now. She needed normal, comforting smells so she could pretend that things were normal and comfortable in her own world, even if they were far from it.

"My heart is broken," Toni began after she'd cried for a bit and finally managed to draw in a deep, shuddering breath. She looked up to Mae and explained in halting words what had happened, more or less.

To her everlasting credit, Mae said nothing, just nodded along with something between sympathy and righteous indignation blossoming on her face as she grasped what Jared had done.

"...and I'm sorry I didn't tell you right away, Mae. I just didn't know how to find the words for it just then."

"Nonsense," Mae said. "You don't owe anything to anybody. Do you hear me? I'll say it again: you don't owe anything to anybody, Toni. Not to your brother or me or to that lousy soon-to-be ex of yours. All you've got to take care of is yourself, okay? Let us handle the rest."

Toni nodded, not willing to trust her voice just yet. Small kindnesses felt like they were being magnified a million times over, to the point where she started crying all over again just because of how it looked like Mae was feeling Toni's pain right along with her. It felt good to know that she wasn't alone. That her family was at her side.

"You sit right there," Mae instructed with a firm point at the chair Toni was in. "I'm going to be right back out, okay?"

Toni nodded again. Mae strode inside. Toni heard doors open and slam, some muffled voices, and the clinking of something from the kitchen.

Then Mae reemerged with a mischievous twinkle in her eye. "I put Eliza in charge of the house for a little while. You and I, darling, are going for a night walk on the beach. And I brought a surprise for the road as well." She waggled a silver flask in front of her face.

"Please tell me that's something strong," Toni said in a hoarse laugh.

"Henry's finest," Mae said with a wink. "He's going to be livid when he finds out I dipped into his liquor cabinet."

"He'll get over it," Toni replied. She wiped her eyes and rose, then followed Mae off the porch and out onto the road.

They walked quietly for a while, passing the whiskey back and forth. Each nip from the flask burned like hellfire going down Toni's throat, but as it settled into her stomach, she felt some of that warm, homey glow diffusing throughout her once again. The soul-shiver seemed to retreat.

It was nice to pad silently through the night. They peeked into the windows of the homes they passed, seeing families at dinner, sprawled on the couch watching TV, all laughter and smiles. Those houses were safe havens from emotions like the heartbreak that Toni was suffering from. She envied them for it, and at the same time, she felt glad that such places existed. In a world as big and random and cruel as this one, it was a good thing that there were oases that could protect folks, even if only for a little while.

She wanted to share those thoughts with Mae, but seeing as how she'd never been much good with words, she didn't know where exactly to start.

"It's always nice being in your home," she said quietly.

"It's your home, too, Toni," Mae answered at once in the same hushed volume.

"I know; you always say so. But it's nice anyway. I just like telling you that."

"Well, thank you, love. Home is a special thing." Mae stopped walking for a second and glanced up. "I don't want to press you on a single thing, darling, and so I'm going to ask you this one time and one time only: do you want to talk about what happened?"

Toni paused as she thought about it. And the more she tossed it around in her head, the more she decided something. "You know what?" she said to Mae. "I honestly don't think I do. Not right now, anyway. Gotta look to the future, or else I'm going to drive myself crazy thinking about the past. I'm sure I'll want to talk about it one day, maybe. But not now."

"I suspected as much," Mae said. She rested her hand on Toni's shoulder. "I won't ever push you again, okay? No sense in bothering you if talking won't fix a darn thing. But just know that I'm here anytime you need me. Forever. We're sisters, right?"

Toni laid her hand on top of Mae's and smiled. "Sisters for life."

Mae nodded, satisfied, and they resumed their walk. They made their way out to the beach and sat there for a while as they finished the last of the whiskey.

Toni started hiccupping by the time they got to the bottom of the flask. She was never a big drinker of strong liquor. Tonight seemed like a good occasion for it, to be sure, but it was doing a number on her nonetheless.

They sat in the soft sand and watched the waves for a while. "I always thought the ocean was so beautiful at night," Toni said.

"Like black glass," agreed Mae.

Eventually, they decided it was time to meander back home. They leaned on each other for support, since both were a little woozier from the whiskey than they had been on the way out.

A few blocks away from Mac's house, Toni saw a dilapidated building seated towards the back of a big, overgrown lot. "Bit of an eyesore, isn't that?" she commented.

Mae glanced over sleepily. "Oh, that one? Yes, it is. It needs quite a lot of work, but I always thought it had nice bones."

They kept walking. Toni looked over at the crumbling home once more before they rounded the corner and it disappeared from sight.

The house was silent when they approached. Toni bid Mae good night as her sister-in-law went to check on the kids, then mounted the stairs and collapsed into her bed.

Sleep came quickly, and when it did, she surrendered herself up to it with gratitude.

# 12

It feels lately as though the days are slipping one right into the next like the steps of a tango, with hardly a pause to differentiate them.

Without even realizing it was happening, Toni has fallen into a rhythm, the facsimile of something that looks—*gasp*—just like a happy, normal life. She eats, she shops, she daydreams. She drinks coffee at cafés with Camille, and she goes to museums with Nicolas.

And at night, they dance.

They dance in just about every *milonga* in the city, it feels like. As Toni gets her sea legs under her, she starts to feel more and more comfortable with all the pageantry that comes along with the art and science of tango in Buenos Aires.

Heck, part of her even starts to like it. After all, there are so many things to like.

Such as the hushed pitter-patter of nervous talking from the newbies as they mingle with the suave, self-assured, hypermasculine locals who charge into the night's venue in search of tourist women to sweep off their feet.

Or the tangled cloud of perfume and cologne that rises over the crowd, so that every step of the dance brings her swirling into exotic scents gathered from every corner of the world.

She likes the music and the athleticism of it, how her feet ache after a long night of dancing. She likes how it feels to step chest to chest with her partner and to feel like there is a kind of primal tête-à-tête between two bodies taking place that doesn't require either person to say a word.

She almost always dances with Nicolas. Each time they dance together, they get better—a little flourish added here, a twirl there—until they have begun to anticipate each other perfectly. By now, all it takes is a raise of the eyebrows or a flash of the eyes to communicate what comes next. In no time at all, Toni has become confident on the dance floor.

Sometimes, though, Nicolas tells her to go dance with someone else. He takes a seat on the edge of the circle for a *tanda* and watches her with laughing eyes.

"Don't you get jealous?" she asks him every now and then when he suggests the idea. "Watching me in the arms of another man?"

He shakes his head, chuckles, and says the same thing every time: "It is a gift to watch you at all, *bella*. Art can be admired from a distance."

It is, as she has come to learn, a classically Nicolas answer—a little mysterious, a little haughty, a lot to love in it. She relishes those moments when he tosses off something so effortlessly poetic. It makes her shiver and smile at the same time.

He means what he says about the art, too. For all that he gives off the appearance of a gruff, no-nonsense businessman, Toni has seen him countless times plant himself in front of a painting at one of Buenos Aires's many astounding art museums for long, unblinking stretches. Just looking, chin in hand, contemplating, observing, letting it all soak in.

Or so he claims. Toni thinks that sometimes he's maybe jerking her chain a little bit and he's really just daydreaming about the errands he has yet to run.

"You don't have to pretend to be so deep, you know," she teases him today. He's standing in front of a massive, grim-looking oil by Francisco Goya, his feet planted wide like a sailor on a ship being tossed by the waves.

This early in the afternoon on a weekday, they pretty much have the place to themselves. Nicolas is playing hooky from work for an hour so they can walk around the museum unencumbered by gawking tourists.

"Deep?" he says, putting a hand on his chest in mock offense. "Me? I am as shallow as the Mississippi, I'm afraid."

"Have you ever even seen the Mississippi?"

"It is an idiom, Toni Benson."

"Mhmm. Whatever you say, you *artista*." She pirouettes away before he can reach out and grab her. He growls in pretend frustration as she giggles and leaves him behind to move into the next room.

There's no one else in here, either. She wanders idly between sculptures carved from black marble, each set on a pedestal and encased in glass. The silence in here is warm and comfortable, a refuge from the bustling, chattering city that surges outside these walls.

She senses rather than hears Nicolas step through the archway to join her in this room.

"Do you think the art ever gets lonely?" she calls to him without looking back over her shoulder.

"Lonely?"

"Yeah. Like at night, you know? It's all quiet, a little boring. They don't get to see much of the world anymore."

She's only joking, of course, but—and this is another thing she loves about Nicolas—sometimes her sarcasm slips beneath his radar. Or maybe he just chooses to weigh her silly thoughts seriously.

Either way, when she glances up, she sees him holding his chin in his hand again, brows furrowed in deep concentration.

Toni laughs. "Don't tell me you're actually sitting here considering the lonely plight of the sculptures, Nicolas." She walks up to him and places a hand on his chest. "It was just a little joke, that's all."

"I was just thinking about how we could break them out of here, actually," he says as his face splits into a wide smile. "You could tuck this little guy here in your purse, right? We'll take him out dancing, maybe."

Toni turns to look at the sculpture in question. It's of a warrior bearing a shield and spear, with rough-hewn facial features that communicate a harsh, stoic seriousness—the same kind she often sees in Nicolas, as a matter of fact.

"I'm not so sure he'd like to tango," she says. She places her chin in her hand, just like Nicolas is doing. "He looks like he has stiff hips, don't you think?"

Nicolas chuckles, a deep rumbling sound that is as welcome as it is rare. "You might be right about that. Besides," he says, turning to face Toni and pulling towards him by her hips, "I think I want you all to myself tonight."

"Is that so?"

"It is very so," Nicolas responds. "And in fact, it is so very so that I want you all to myself this weekend, too. Take a trip with me."

"A trip?"

"Just a short one. We'll go to Tigre, down the river in Uruguay. It's a beautiful little town. You'll love it."

"Oh, so now *I'm* the one being sprung out of this museum and taken to see the world, hm?"

Nicolas laughs again. "If that is how you choose to see things, who am I to tell you differently?"

"Nobody special, that's for sure," Toni says. She can only hold her faux-serious scowl for a second before she bursts out laughing and touches Nicolas on the chest again. "Kidding, kidding."

"And here I was getting ready to start crying."

"Oh God, let's not. I don't think I'm ready for that. Big hairy man tears would terrify me."

"Am I not allowed to cry, Toni?"

"What would you be crying about?"

"Well, you haven't said yes to my trip proposal yet."

Toni rolls her eyes and extricates herself from Nicolas's embrace. "For crying out loud, yes, of course! You are such a drama queen, I swear." But she's laughing as she spins away and moves into the next room.

They spend the next half hour holding hands, not saying much of anything aside from "Look at this one" or "Did you see...?" It is as perfect an afternoon as Toni can remember. When they reemerge from the museum, the three o'clock sun is bright and hot.

"Having summer in November will never stop being weird," Toni grumbles as she fans herself. "It's backward."

Nicolas grins wickedly. He knows well that life in the southern hemisphere throws Toni for a loop every now and then, and he relishes making her confront it. "Nothing like a Christmastime suntan, right?" he says.

She thwacks him on the shoulder. "Leave me be, you pest."

"Never." He swoops in and kisses her. "But this is your life now, no?"

"What do you mean?"

"You live here," he says, spreading a hand to encompass the whole city. "Heat in November is how things are."

"Sure," she laughs. "For now."

"What do *you* mean?"

She shrugs. "Well, whenever I go back home, things will be right again."

To her surprise, Nicolas frowns. She hadn't meant anything by the comment, but it seems to have landed awkwardly. "Right," he says under his breath.

She's sorely tempted to ask what is going on inside his big handsome head. But they'd been having such a nice afternoon until now, and it feels like they might be angling towards a fight if she pursues it.

So, instead, she rises up to her tiptoes and kisses him again. "Cheer up, Grinch," she says.

"Grinch?"

"Like the movie?"

"I don't..."

She shakes her head in disbelief. "Ah, jeez, never mind. We have a lot of work to do with you."

He is still smiling as he checks his watch. "Perhaps we do. Unfortunately, duty calls for now."

Toni kisses him lightly on the cheek. "Better get to it then."

"How can I go look at shipping invoices when I know that a pretty woman waits for me?"

"Who said I'm waiting for you?" It's her turn to grin wickedly.

"A man can hope, I suppose. All right then, off I go." He kisses her on the cheek, squeezes her hand once, and then saunters off to find the nearest subway station to convey him back to his offices.

Toni stands on the steps of the museum and watches him go. He cuts a handsome figure among the crowd. Half a head taller and twice as good looking as all the others, or so it seems to her. And that pride in his step—it used to irk her. That's a funny memory. Nowadays, it just makes her laugh.

When he descends down the steps into the station, she sighs, readjusts her purse strap on her shoulder, and sets off to find a café for a little snack and some reading. She doesn't stop smiling for the rest of the afternoon.

~

### TWO DAYS LATER

The wind in Toni's face is salty and refreshing. She keeps a tight grip on the handrail as she looks out over the surface of the water. Nicolas's hand rests gently on her lower back, too. She looks up at him.

"Worried I'm going to fall overboard?" she inquires with a twinkle in her eye.

"I'd dive in after you," he says immediately and earnestly.

"Would you tread water in the Arctic for me?"

He turns to look at her with a quizzical slant to his eyebrows. "Hm?"

"Be the Jack to my Rose?"

"You're doing it again," he comments dryly.

Toni gasps. "Don't tell me you haven't seen *Titanic*!"

"Like the ship?"

She claps her hands to her cheeks in mock horror. "This is a sin. We need to rectify that immediately, for the sake of your mortal soul."

"Ah well, that's a lost cause anyway, so let's not worry about it."

Toni's laugh turns into a squeal as the ferry boat conveying them from Buenos Aires down the Luján River to the cozy village of Tigre hits a patch of turbulence in the water and nearly throws her overboard.

"I told you to keep a hand on the rail," Nicolas warns when she's found her balance again.

"Oh hush. I was fine. Who needs a Jack anyway?"

In response, Nicolas pulls her close and plants a kiss on top of her head. It's a perfect answer.

They pull into the docks an hour later. The sun is setting over the land behind them as they disembark, suitcases in hand, and find a car waiting for them. It's a short ride to the woodsy cabin that Nicolas has rented for the weekend.

The driver helps them shepherd their suitcases indoors, then leaves them alone. Toni wanders around to check the place out.

It's a wooden cabin set on stilts to elevate it above the low waters of the river that flow beneath the home. Everything inside is done up in well-crafted blond wood that gleams with varnish. The walls are festooned with tapestries and the homey patina of years' and years' worth of collectibles—family heirlooms, bits of jewelry, pots and pans and pieces of art.

Toni is about to turn to tell Nicolas how warm and fuzzy it makes her feel, when a sudden thought hits her with a lurch in the stomach.

A cabin on the water. Why does that feel so familiar?

And then she remembers.

Jared.

How many years ago was it that she thought a cabin on the water would be her salvation, the resurrection of her love, the savior of her marriage?

That was another Toni. But life has brought her back here. And, as much as she tries to quell the sensation, she begins to feel a head-pounding nausea and a ringing in her ears. It's a budding panic attack, completely unwanted and yet insistent on making itself felt.

*Breathe,* Toni tries to tell herself, but since when has that ever worked? She says it again and again as the ringing grows louder and her head pounds harder.

Maybe there was no escaping what fate or God or whatever has always had in mind for her. One way or another, she's spent a lifetime trying to escape the gravitational pull of the sorrow that seems to keep following her. She thought that, with Nicolas, she'd finally achieved that. She'd broken free of all that grief, all that sadness.

And then she found herself here, and she realized that maybe she hadn't broken free of anything. She'd just been deluding herself all along. It's a stupid, irrational thought, but that's the stuff that her panic attacks have always been made of. A cabin is just a cabin, right?

Wrong. Tell that to her trembling body, her racing brain.

Her head is pounding, her palms are sweating, her heart is racing, and she's just about to turn and tell Nicolas that she's sorry, but she has to leave, she needs to get out of this cabin and this country and go back home, because what was she even thinking of doing here, with him? How dare she hope?

Then a gentle hand caresses her neck.

When it does, it's as if Nicolas's touch is a syringe withdrawing poison from her veins. It's magic, and it would seem borderline ridiculous if it weren't actually happening right here and right now. If she read this in a book or saw it in a movie—*He touched her, and everything was perfect, and they lived happily ever after*—she would've certainly rolled her eyes and gone looking for a different story altogether.

This isn't quite that. But it is closer than she ever dared dream was possible. Because she realizes something when Nicolas touches her: She is safe here. She is loved here. Nicolas isn't Jared, and Jared isn't Nicolas, and she is no longer the Toni she once was.

She's been through things. Tragedies and triumphs, heartbreaks and hopes. To be here at all is a victory.

All she has to do is open her eyes and see that.

She turns to Nicolas. Before he can say anything, she throws herself at him and kisses him hard on the lips.

Lord, does it feel good.

$\sim$

The sun filtering through the blinds the next morning is softer than it has any right to be, not that Toni is complaining. She's slept deeply, and even now, she is in no particular hurry to wake up.

Nicolas's side of the bed is empty, though when she reaches over and feels it, she notices that it is still warm. Just as she is frowning, wondering where he's gone, he darkens the doorway.

She looks up. He is smiling at her with a cup of steaming coffee in each hand. Shirtless, too, she notices with a flirtatious smile. His insistence on doing one hundred push-ups and one hundred sit-ups every single morning, no matter the time or place or how much Toni begs him to just stay in bed and pillow-talk with her, serves him well.

"Looking for me?" he asks.

"Never," she denies. "I was just eyeing your side of the bed. Feels softer. Did you manipulate me into taking the thinner pillows, too?"

"You wound me with your suspicion, *señorita,*" he says as he paces over and hands Toni her cup of coffee.

She takes it gratefully. "I never know with you," she says as she eyes him over the rim of the mug. "Always up to something."

"Funny you should say that." He sinks back into bed. "I actually need to stay here for a bit today and make a few calls. You should go into town and explore for a while."

"Make a few calls? Very vague, very suspicious. What're you up to?"

He gives her a pleasant grin. "Don't be so paranoid. Just business. The details would bore you."

"Oh, I dunno about that," Toni muses. "I love details."

"Not these, I promise."

"Fine," she pouts. "You're kicking me out of the house so you can do something mysterious. I'll allow it, but I'm onto you, mister."

"I'd certainly hope so." With a sudden flash of movement, he sets his coffee down and bears down on Toni's neck with a flurry of kisses, tickling her at the same time.

An hour later, she finds herself wandering through a cute bohemian district downtown, still feeling the lingering ghost of those kisses on her neck and cheek and smiling at the memory.

Nicolas gave her a few suggestions on things to check out. So, after securing a quick bite to eat at a charming little coffee shop, she goes to check out the art district.

The day passes by easily. She is in no rush to be anywhere in particular, so she takes her time in each of the shops, chatting with the owners and perusing all the paintings they have on display. She ends up with three or four pieces of art tucked into cardboard tubes under her arm.

Being an innkeeper for so long, she developed a serious weakness for local trinkets and souvenirs. Her guests brought her things from all around the world, and she loved touching them and imagining the journeys each little piece had been on.

She thinks of her beloved inn, of Mae and the kids, and wonders how they are doing. She ought to call again soon and check in. It's been a little while since she last spoke to her sister-in-law.

Eventually, four o'clock rolls around. Nicolas texts her that he will be finishing up momentarily, so she has the all-clear to come back to the cabin.

After navigating her way back to the cabin, she smells something strange as she walks up the steps. It's oddly familiar. But she can't place it until she opens the door and sees everything inside.

"Surprise!" Nicolas greets.

Toni's jaw drops. "Oh. My. Lord."

Spread out on the kitchen table is a Thanksgiving feast for two. A big, brined turkey, mashed potatoes, slices of cranberry sauce…it looks like something right off the cover of *Bon Appetit* magazine. She almost wonders whether the food is fake. But when she drops the cardboard tubes and runs her finger around the rim of the bowl of mashed potatoes, she feels the heat. She sticks her finger in her mouth and relishes the taste.

"Oh my Lord," she repeats.

"You said that already."

"I'll say it again, too! Nico, what did you *do?*"

He smiles, the thousand-megawatt smile she loves seeing on him. "I know you have missed home. And it is Thanksgiving, or so I hear. So I whipped a little something up."

She gazes again at the full spread. "'A little something'? Who taught you how to make turkey, for crying out loud?"

He shrugs, a little sheepish. "I may have consulted one or two YouTube videos."

"Nico, it's...it's..." She looks up at him. Her eyes and heart are both full. "It's amazing."

She didn't know she'd been missing home quite as badly as the pang in her chest would suggest. The sight of this food in this place makes her heart twinge with affection for Nantucket, for November snow flurries out the window and a house bursting with family and rich smells. Those are good things, yes, and she misses them terribly.

But that isn't even the real thing of it all.

What is getting to her even more is that he would do all this for her. That he cares. That he—*gulp*—likes her? Loves her? She doesn't know which words are right in any of the languages Nicolas speaks.

That doesn't matter so much, though. As she stares at Nicolas, biting her lip to hold back happy tears, she knows that he wouldn't care which words she picked. They fell for each other while dancing— hardly a word spoken between them. And it seems that the most important moments that pass between them are always the silent ones.

So she decides she doesn't need to say much of anything at all. She walks up to him and squeezes his hand, then stands on her tiptoes to kiss him on the lips.

He is a good man. He is her man.

That's enough.

# 13

Toni woke up with a dry mouth and a headache lodged deep in her temples. She stayed in bed, staring at the ceiling with gummy eyelids as she groaned softly.

"I am way too old to be getting hangovers," she mumbled to no one in particular.

She heard the pitter-patter of young footsteps scampering up and down the stairs over and over again. Those belonged to Brent, no doubt, who appeared to be off to a rowdy start on this bright and sunny morning. From what she could make out through the door, it sounded like he was miming fireworks exploding, complete with the whine, the boom, and the crackling aftermath. *Very on-brand for the little hellion*, Toni thought to herself.

She wasn't sure how long she lay there, thinking about nothing in particular before she decided that lazing about in bed was going to do precisely zero favors for her future prospects.

What to do, though?

A shower and breakfast seemed like a reasonable place to start. She let out a hiss as she sat upright and threw the covers off her. The motion caused her headache to rear up fiercely. Easy does it, then—no need to rush the day.

She hobbled her way to the adjoined bathroom, found a towel in the linen closet, and got the shower going. She stood and looked in the mirror as she waited for the water to warm up.

"Well, old girl," she said to herself, feeling a little silly for talking at her reflection but much too hungover to care, "you've got what you wanted. A fresh start, wasn't that it? Isn't that what you asked for?"

Her baleful eyes gazed back. They were still red and weary from last night's whiskey, which had kicked her in the teeth a little harder than she'd realized until she and Mae had begun the walk back.

What she was saying was true; a fresh start was exactly what she'd voiced to the universe. But the one she had in mind looked nothing like this. So much for hot coffee and summer sunrises over the lake with her husband in the rocking chair next to her. So much for the chirping of birds getting their day started. Instead, she was camped out in her niece's bedroom while her nephew stormed around outside, now pretending to be a tiger.

"A real monkey's paw situation you've found yourself in, Toni," she scowled. Her reflection scowled right back. "Isn't this the part where you say, 'I never should have made that stupid wish?'"

She wrangled her hair into some semblance of neatness. The first curls of steam from the shower had begun to seep out, although Toni had spent enough nights here to know that the hot water was never in any hurry to arrive. She still had another minute or two before the shower would be bearable. Long enough to castigate her image in the mirror a bit more, at least.

"Here's the thing, though: maybe this was all for the best. Could be, couldn't it?"

Her voice was hopeful—far too hopeful for her to actually believe the words she was saying. She knew she was trying to convince herself that this was all headed towards a happily ever after.

But right here and right now, it sure didn't feel that way. It felt a lot closer to rock bottom.

*Enough,* she thought to herself. She tried it out loud: "Enough."

She needed to quit it with the self-pity, with the wallowing in her own muck. The recurring thought that was troubling her most was that her future was wide-open and empty. What she ought to do instead was figure out what kinds of things might fill it.

She thought of the house she and Mae had passed on their way home from the beach last night. It was like the seed of an idea, one that didn't have any shape just yet. Toni couldn't quite say *why* she thought of that house; all she knew was that there was something to it that was appealing.

She also thought of Mae's comment that her old friend Kendra Adkins had just given birth to a little girl. "Bingo!" she said out loud. "I'll swing by for a visit today." What better than a newborn to cheer her up?

She felt the familiar pang of sadness that she always felt whenever a new birth announcement made its way to her through the grapevine. *When will it be my turn?* went the self-pitying complaint.

But now was not the time for that. She had more concrete things to mourn for right now.

When she saw a bead of sweat form on her forehead, she knew the shower was ready. She stepped in. It felt good to rinse off the crustiness of the hangover, and her headache felt a little better by the time she was scrubbed, toweled off, dressed, and on her way downstairs to see what wonders Mae's kitchen might be holding this morning. The fresh smell of coffee hit her before she even got to the bottom of the staircase.

"Which of my gremlins is that?" Mae called out from around the corner. She smiled when Toni came into sight. "Oh! Sorry, Toni. Not a gremlin at all."

"Don't be so sure," Toni said with a wink. "Could I bother you for an aspirin, hon?"

Mae grinned and pointed with her spatula towards a hallway closet. "Third shelf in there, little red bottle. Did the whiskey fight back?"

"It is certainly trying its best," Toni admitted sheepishly as she followed Mae's directions and retrieved a white miracle pill. "As if I needed the reminder for why I stick to wine."

"Shall I add a little brandy to your coffee, then?" Mae said with a wicked smile when Toni returned to her stool behind the kitchen counter. "Hair of the dog?"

"Only if you want to see a sad old woman get sick all over your kitchen."

Mae swatted Toni on the elbow. "If you're old, that means I'm old, and I don't want to be old, so stop saying that."

Toni smiled again. She drank gratefully from the cup of coffee Mae placed in front of her. It warmed her bones as soon as it went down, and the headache receded just a bit further.

"Over-medium eggs on rye toast, right?" Mae asked with the wry air of someone who already knew that she was right.

"One of these days, I'm going to deprive you of the pleasure of knowing the right thing to do in every single circumstance," Toni teased. "But yes, eggs and toast sound like a gift from the gods. What did I do to deserve a sister-in-law like you?"

Mae chuckled as she expertly cracked two eggs onto the skillet. Their sizzle rang out pleasantly in the morning air. "You must've been someone special indeed in a former life." She winked. "Only joking. I might ask you the same question, actually."

Toni barked out a shallow laugh. "Ah yes, I'm exactly what everyone is always begging for: an unexpected house guest arriving on short notice to eat your food and steal your daughter's bedroom."

Sara came wandering into the kitchen blearily just then, before Mae could say something pointed about Toni's poor attitude this morning. "Good morning, hon," Toni greeted her niece. "Sleep okay?"

"Well, if it isn't Sleeping Beauty!" Mae exclaimed sarcastically. "Or are you the Scarecrow from *The Wizard of Oz*? With that hair, I'm not so sure!"

Sara's blonde hair was sticking up in all directions, and it did look an awful lot like a messily assembled straw man. Toni figured she'd stay quiet on this particular topic, though, judging by the acidic grimace on Sara's face at her mom's cheery early morning jesting.

"Ha. Ha. Ha," Sara intoned grumpily. "Coffee, please."

"Lord, child, you think you're just so grown!" Mae said, wide-eyed with her hands on her hips. "You know the rules: no coffee until you're older."

"But Mom, that's not fair!" Sara whined. "Jenny MacMillan's mom lets her drink coffee on the weekends whenever she wants!"

"Well, hip hooray for Jenny MacMillan," Mae shot back without hesitation. "Do let me know if you decide to move into their house. I'll be sure to inform Mrs. MacMillan that you snore at night."

"Ugh!" Sara yelped. She threw up her hands and stormed out of the room, fuming.

Mae winked at Toni once her daughter was gone. "Life with teenage daughters is wonderful, isn't it?"

"She's headstrong, that one," Toni acknowledged.

"Has been since the day she was born. And it's only getting worse. I fear that our worst years might be ahead of us, as far as mother-to-daughter communications go."

"I don't envy you that," said Toni. "Speaking of daughters, I think I'm going to go say hello to Kendra and her husband today. Are they still at the same house?"

"Oh yes," Mae said, "I believe so. Here, eat this," she slid the finished eggs and toast over in front of Toni, "and I'll go put together a little gift basket for you to bring to them."

"Oh," interrupted Toni, "you don't have to—" But Mae was already gone, whisking away down the hallway to rummage through closets and singing softly to herself all the while.

Toni laughed. Mae Benson was a good match for her brother, that was for sure. The woman could hold her own no matter the storm she was facing. It was reassuring to see her poise and calmness in the midst of the chaos that came with running a house of four Benson children. Toni felt like she was drawing a little strength from her example—or perhaps from her cooking; it was hard to say which was helping more.

By the time Toni had finished eating—and the hangover had admitted it was fighting a losing battle against her sister-in-law's peerless good grace—Mae had assembled a small wicker basket filled with flowers, candy, and a bottle of wine. "That last one is for the parents," she said with a teasing elbow to Toni's side.

"I can't promise it will make it to them," joked Toni.

Mae looked up with a mixture of amusement and concern in her eyes. "Hey there," she said softly, in the kind of voice that Toni understood meant she was talking indirectly about the crumbling of her marriage. "Whatever it takes, you know?" She squeezed Toni's forearm tenderly. "Tell Kendra I said hello."

"Will do," Toni replied after a moment. She felt a little choked up. Small gestures like Mae's carried outsized importance these days. Everything had been flipped upside down. The thought of Jared was just too big to process, so she felt numb whenever he crossed her mind. But a pair of eggs on rye, the simple touch of Mae's fingertips on the back of her hand? Those things meant everything.

"And Mae?"

"Yes, love?"

"Thank you."

Mae paused in the hallway for a moment before she turned around and smiled at Toni once more. "I'll tell you something my momma always used to say to me: I'd give you the world in a handbasket if I could, darling." She cleared her throat. "But seeing as how I can't, you'll have to settle for the wine."

~

Kendra's house had hardly changed at all from the last time she'd been here. That must've been at least five years ago.

It seemed a shame to Toni that they'd lost contact. Life just got in the way, she supposed. Through no fault on either end, they'd simply talked less and less until they fell off altogether. Calls went unreturned, Christmas cards didn't get mailed, and before she knew it, her friendship had dissipated.

And where had that left her? When Jared did what he did, did Toni have an army of friends waiting to take up torches and pitchforks on her behalf?

Not as many as she might have once upon a time. Looking back on it now, it seemed crazy not to be more diligent about those things. Kendra and dozens of other friends had gradually slipped away into lives of their own when Toni had forgotten to keep looking out for them.

She needed those friendships. Pity that she was just now realizing it, but better late than never, right? They'd sustained her in a way she didn't realize was vital. Female friendships—that's what made the world go 'round. That had to be a song lyric or something. A fortune cookie saying, maybe.

Toni was thankful for the basket that Mae had bundled together for her. She would've felt horribly guilty showing up unannounced and empty-handed. She hadn't even known that Kendra was pregnant, after all! This, at least, let her come knocking with a shred of dignity intact. As it was, she felt a little bit nervous as she parked her bicycle at the end of the driveway and walked up to Kendra's front door.

Like just about every other family home on the island, the outside was done up in that classic Nantucket gray. It looked placid and friendly in the midmorning sunlight, and the emerald green of the hedges and lawn was a nice contrast.

Kendra had fresh flowers blooming in windowsill pots, Toni saw. Which made sense, seeing as how she ran a florist's shop she inherited from her parents. She had a natural touch for making things grow around her. Even when they were in high school, Toni remembered how Kendra had been forever fostering things—birds with broken wings, runaway cats with independent streaks, the tomato vines they were assigned for a freshman-year biology project.

She rang the doorbell and waited. She shifted her weight back and forth from foot to foot. The sudden nervousness that had overtaken her didn't seem to come from anywhere in particular, but it didn't exactly require Sherlock Holmes to figure out why her palms had begun to sweat and her lingering hangover had returned with a vengeance.

In a cruel way, she was about to open the door on a picture of what her life might have been like if everything had gone according to plan. Mae had mentioned at dinner that Kendra and her husband, Andy, were the spitting image of happy and in love. With a newborn daughter to grace their home, Toni had no doubt that they would be radiating happy energy.

She wished she could reciprocate. As she stood on the threshold listening to the footsteps approach from within, she did her best to project the kind of peace and vitality she was desperately wishing for herself.

Then the door swung open.

It took a moment for Kendra to recognize her old friend, but Toni had no trouble at all. Both women split into broad smiles at the exact same moment and squealed excitedly.

"Toni Bologna!"

"Kenzie!"

They embraced. Toni felt a little silly for her girlish yelp, but oh well —it was okay to be a little silly sometimes, wasn't it?

"Oh my God, I can't believe it's you!" Kendra exclaimed when they'd parted ways, though she didn't quite let go of Toni's forearm. "You look amazing."

"I should say the same to you!" Toni took in Kendra's long, dirty blonde curls, which fell almost all the way down to her waist. Between the healthy hair and the watermelon-pink sundress she was wearing, she was practically glowing.

"Come in, come in!" Kendra said, dragging Toni inside. "I'm still in shock. Where did you come from? It's so good to see you."

"I'm in town for the Fourth," Toni explained as she followed Kendra to the living room. "My sister-in-law told me that you'd recently had a baby, so I thought I'd swing by to say hello. I'm sorry for just dropping in on you like this—I forgot your phone number, if I'm being perfectly honest. I felt terrible."

"Don't even start!" Kendra snapped cheerily. "I couldn't be happier to see you. It has been way, way too long. Can I get you anything? Lemonade? Water? Coffee? It's a little early to start drinking, unless...?"

"No, no," Toni said in horror. She raised a hand to ward off the merest thought of alcohol as she blanched with a wave of nausea. "Mae and I stole a little bit of Henry's whiskey last night, so alcohol is the last thing on my mind, believe me."

Kendra chuckled. She had a beautiful, feminine laugh, like tinkling bells. It went perfectly hand in hand with the glow of her hair and the pop of the colors she favored in her clothes. "Water it is, then."

"That would be lovely, thank you."

Toni sank back into the leather armchair as Kendra went into the kitchen and filled a pair of glasses with cool water and ice. She accepted it gratefully when her friend came back.

"You're a lifesaver, Kendra. My body can't handle drinking anymore."

"I'll drink to that," Kendra laughed again, raising her water glass in a mock toast. "Those days are far behind us. Lord, we used to be able to get into all kinds of trouble and still show up bright-eyed and bushy-tailed at school, didn't we, though?"

"Here's to being eighteen again," agreed Toni with a smile.

Kendra shook her head. "Oh, you couldn't pay me enough to go back to that age. My thirties suit me much better."

"You look fantastic, hon. How's motherhood?"

"Well, I'm only a month in and still getting my sea legs back under me after the delivery. But honestly, I'm loving it." Kendra leaned forward so that Toni caught sight of how her eyes were glistening with happiness. "She's an angel, full stop. Sleeping about as well as can be expected, but how can I complain when I get to wake up four times a night to that cute little face?"

"Where is the bundle of joy?"

"Andy just took her for a walk around the block—get some fresh air, you know—so they should be back any second." She glanced at her watch and smiled.

The whole scene made Toni want to laugh and cry at the same time. Here was someone she'd grown up with, gotten in trouble with, dealt with high school crushes and heartbreak and first loves with, coming into full bloom as a mother and a wife. It was beautiful to see.

But, at the same time, Kendra's light made Toni feel so small and shadowy. It wasn't quite accurate to call it envy, though it was certainly a cousin of it. Longing might be a better word, with a wistful bent to it. She wanted Kendra's happiness, not her circumstances, necessarily. She wanted to feel like she belonged somewhere. Like she had purpose. She wanted to care for people and be cared for in return. Surely that wasn't such a bad thing?

"And, speaking of Andy, how are the two of you?"

Kendra touched Toni's knee and smiled even wider. "He's the best. I don't know how on earth I got so lucky, but he's taken to fatherhood like a fish out of water. He pops out of bed before my eyes even open the second that Maggie starts fussing, he changes diapers, he makes bottles—he's Super Dad, really."

"You picked good," said Toni.

"I did. I really did. I just feel—like, blessed, you know? But, anyway, I'm rambling on and on, so rude of me! Tell me about you. Tell me everything, tell me now. I missed you!"

Toni had known this was coming. Anyone would—it's the natural kind of question that you ask of a friend you haven't seen in a long time. And yet, she'd been sort of hoping, sort of praying that it wouldn't come up, that she'd be able to swoop in and more or less warm herself by the fireside of Kendra and Andy's happy little family and then leave without having to dampen their light with scraps of her own budding misery. It was a foolish hope, she knew, but one she'd been clinging to nonetheless.

"I—" she started to say.

But then, like a prayer being fulfilled, the front door swung open. Andy came in with one-month-old Maggie in his arms, and Kendra's question was immediately forgotten.

"Oh my goodness!" Toni yelped as she jumped to her feet. "Kendra, you have outdone yourself. She is absolutely gorgeous." Toni would've said that no matter what, of course, but it was made much easier by the fact that it was one hundred percent true.

"Our little Gerber baby," Andy joked as he bobbled his daughter playfully. "Gonna bring home those modeling bucks to Mommy and Daddy, yeah? Buy us a yacht?"

Kendra rolled her eyes, and Toni laughed as they all gathered together in the foyer. "Honey, you remember Toni Benson, right?"

"Of course!" Andy said. He switched Maggie from the crook of one elbow to the other and shook Toni's hand. "How are you?"

He was a handsome guy, with dark, mussy hair and an easy smile, the kind of face that immediately sets a person at ease. His handshake was like his personality—warm, comforting, gentle. And, just like Kendra, he was practically bursting with exuberance.

"Not as good as the two of you, apparently," said Toni. "The three of you, I should say. You guys should be on the front of a family life magazine or something."

Andy grinned and looked to his wife. "Did you hear that, babe? She thinks we're cover models. Maybe the two of you. I was always told I had a face for radio, though."

"Ignore him," instructed Kendra through a smile. "He thinks he's funny."

"I'm in trouble, aren't I?" Andy asked Toni. "Outnumbered by the women now. My days of getting some respect in this house are extremely numbered."

"You might want to practice your 'Yes, darling,' and curtsy right now," Toni quipped.

"Don't I know it. Can I get you anything?"

"Kendra's got me all set, but thank you so much."

He nodded, still beaming. "Well, she hasn't gotten you this yet, has she?" Then, with no fanfare whatsoever, he plunked Maggie into Toni's arms, winked, and walked past them into the kitchen to wash his hands.

Toni was frozen stiff as a board for a second before she finally came to her senses and looked down at the little angel she was holding. Her eyes were the clearest glacier blue that Toni had ever seen, that translucent otherworldly shade that only newborns have. Between that and her long, dark eyelashes, Toni was ready to weep at the little girl's beauty in those first few seconds already.

"She looks sleepy," Toni murmured. Indeed, Maggie's eyes were fluttering open and closed, like she wanted badly to look back and figure out just who this Toni woman was, but couldn't quite muster up the alertness to do it.

"Just about naptime," said Kendra.

Toni brushed the tenderest finger she could against Maggie's tiny nose. "She is perfect."

"Says someone who clearly doesn't change her diapers!" Andy called from the kitchen.

"She is a lot of work," Kendra agreed, "even if we do love her."

"Like a fixer-upper, you know?" Andy chimed in again as he rejoined them. "Always something to tend to, and just when you think you're all set, the roof caves in. Or something like that, I don't know. I was never much good at analogies."

"This is why you should stick to computers, dear," Kendra said with a gentle wifely smile.

"Sage advice. Speaking of which, I've gotta go answer a couple emails real quick. Paternity leave, shmaternity leave, am I right? Someone needs to explain the concept to my boss." He bid Toni a quick goodbye and disappeared into the back of the house.

Toni and Kendra sat back down in the living room and talked for a while more. Toni kept perfectly still so as not to jostle the sleeping Maggie while they reminisced about high school and gossiped about how everyone they'd known growing up was turning out—babies and weddings and divorces and new businesses, that kind of thing. Miraculously, they managed to stay away from Toni's personal life, until at long last, Maggie awoke and began to whimper.

"Time for lunch, I think," Kendra said with a scrutinizing eye.

Toni handed Maggie over carefully and stood up. "I think so for me, too. What're you guys doing for the Fourth tomorrow?"

"I think we're going to go down to the beach with my parents. You?"

"Mae and I are going to take the kids down to watch the fireworks from the cove, I believe. Maybe we'll see you there?"

Kendra nodded and smiled. "Sounds lovely. Toni, I can't tell you how good it was to see you. Let's not drift apart again, okay?"

"Pinky promise," said Toni. She hugged her friend once more before letting herself out the front.

She was surprised by something as she went down the steps and retrieved her bike from where she'd left it: she felt a little better than she did before.

And there was something else, too—an idea in the back of her head that was just now beginning to take shape.

# 14

BUENOS AIRES, ARGENTINA—DECEMBER 31, 2018

It is New Year's Eve. Where has the time gone?

It feels like it was only yesterday that Toni was stepping off the plane from Nantucket carrying all kinds of baggage—literal and emotional alike. It feels like it was only yesterday that she was standing in the baggage claim lobby, exhausted and irritated beyond belief, bickering with a strange, angry man in a business suit about whose bag belonged to whom.

Now, that same man is smiling at her like she's the greatest thing he's ever seen. That same man is still wearing a suit, yes, but tonight it is a tuxedo. Rather than hate him on sight, Toni briefly considers the thought that maybe the exact opposite is true: maybe she is falling in love with him.

It's a preposterous thought, and so she shoos it away before it picks up too much momentum. But she knows it's not the last she's seen of it—mostly because it's not the first she's seen of it, either. The thought of whether she might be in love with Nicolas has cropped up again and again over the last month or so like mushrooms after a rain shower.

She thought it first in Tigre, when he stepped aside to reveal a decadent Thanksgiving spread transported there from half a world away. In the days and weeks since, she's thought it more and more.

Simple things make her think it—the way his hands look when he holds a cup of coffee or a pen, so strong and capable. The way he can wink so suavely. The way he laughed when he found out that Toni didn't know how to wink and the way they spent the next two hours together trying (and failing) to teach her.

Subtler things make her think it, too. The sound of his footsteps coming down the hallway of her hotel. How he folds the sheets in the linen closet of his apartment so crisp and neat, almost military-like.

It's a revelation in the strangest way to think those things. Toni has pondered on why that might be, and what she's settled on is this: it is strange to fall in love with Nicolas for those reasons because she never thought that love could make itself felt in such small, insignificant ways before.

She sees it most in his hands, as crazy as that is. They're big and capable, but she's felt their soft touch on her back while they dance and she knows how gentle he can be. Every time Nicolas touches her with those hands, Toni's mind flashes back to the night of Jared's surprise party all those years ago. She remembers Jared's hands balled into fists at his sides and she relives the shock and embarrassment of that moment.

Nicolas would never. But is loving someone's hands actually love?

The more Toni thinks about it, the more Toni decides that it might be the only true form of love there is.

Those same strong, assured hands come to rest lightly on her collarbones. "Are you all right?" Nicolas rumbles. "You look...distracted."

The lights of the awning overhead, a kind of vintage movie theater thing, reflect off his irises as Toni looks up at him. She smiles faintly. "I am here with you," she says.

Nicolas smiles back. "And what a blessing that is." He runs a hand through his dark hair (which has actually begun to show signs of some incoming salt-and-pepperiness, making Nicolas blanch and Toni cackle in delight) and rolls his eyes.

She pinches him on the side. "Don't be sarcastic."

"Ow! I wasn't."

"Sounded sarcastic to me."

"Everything sounds sarcastic to Americans. You are constitutionally incapable of accepting things at face value."

"Don't speak ill of my countrymen," Toni smarms back, hiding a grin. She knows Nicolas hates when she gets faux-patriotic. He usually rolls his eyes and tries to pull out a map to show her that America is, in fact, not the center of the world. She doesn't care much about the whole topic one way or the other—she just likes to push his buttons sometimes, to get him riled up.

"As you wish. Now, are you coming with me, or shall we retreat and go dancing instead?"

Toni swats him on the shoulder. She lets her hand linger a second longer afterward, admiring the taut feel of his muscles. Those push-ups really do wonders for the man.

"Hush, we're not retreating anywhere. This is important for your work, right?"

Nicolas sighs and eyes the inside of the building ruefully. "I suppose it is."

"Then in we go." Toni takes his elbow again, and they stride down the red carpet and into the chic movie theater where the event is being held.

Nicolas's firm has rented the place out for tonight's New Year's Eve gala. It's buzzing with men in tuxedos and women in elegant ballgowns. The chatter of half a dozen different languages rises up in a tumult over the crowd. With Nicolas having so many international clients, it's like the Tower of Babel in here.

Toni smiles. She's come to appreciate the beauty of things she doesn't understand, even if it took some getting used to when she first arrived in Argentina.

A waiter approaches them at once, bearing flutes of golden champagne on a tray. "*Gracias,*" Toni says as gracefully as she can while taking one. She turns to Nicolas and clinks her glass against his. "Happy New Year to us."

"Happy New Year," he murmurs back.

Toni feels a hand brush her shoulder. She turns around to see Camille, and her eyebrows shoot up in glee. "Cami! Oh my goodness, come here." The two women embrace. Toni feels her heart surge with happiness. Food, drinks, friends, celebrations, and the turning of the calendar on one of the most tumultuous years of her life—there is so much to be grateful for this evening, and she is doing her best to throw that gratitude everywhere she can, like rice at a wedding.

"You look ravishing," Camille says with that French shimmer in her voice that gives the word "ravishing" the kind of life it deserves. "Come, come, turn around, let me see it all."

Toni obliges with a devilish grin as she gives her friend a full twirl and runway strut. She is wearing a burnished golden dress that sweeps all the way to the floor from an empire waist. The top is a deep V-neck with wide golden straps over the shoulders. She fell in love at first sight when she saw it on the rack at a shop in San Telmo.

And when Nicolas saw it after she brought it home, he got some mischievous ideas.

"Stunning," Camille repeats after Toni has finished her playful dog-and-pony show, "absolutely stunning."

"You're not so bad yourself, darling!" Toni shoots back. She considers winking and thinks better of it.

Camille looks as exotic and gorgeous as she always does, in a glittering navy dress with long sleeves and a V-cut that swoops all the way down to just above her navel. Her legs look lean and beautiful in the slit up the sides of the dress, and the sparkle coming off her many rings makes the whole ensemble come to life beneath the overhead lights.

"Shall I leave you two ladies to compliment each other back and forth for a while?" Nicolas asks sarcastically.

Camille clucks. "The poor baby is upset that we didn't tell him he's gorgeous! Come here, love. You are a handsome scoundrel, as always."

Toni laughs as Nicolas bends down, scowling, to give Camille the customary kiss on the cheek.

"Now," Camille says when Nicolas's bruised ego has been tended to, "I'm off to find some alcohol. I'll catch up with you two lovebirds in a little while. *Ciao.*" And then she sweeps off, leaving Nicolas and Toni chuckling to one another in her wake.

"She is a shot of life, that one," Toni says.

"A handful."

She gives him a side-eye. "Is that what you say about me behind my back?" she asks in an ominous tone.

Nicolas blanches and looks almost offended. "Of course not!" he exclaims, mortified. Then his face splits into a big, wicked smile. "I say you are *two* handfuls."

Toni yelps and swats him again, with her clutch this time. "You're on thin ice already, mister," she warns him. "I'd be on my best behavior if I were you. Otherwise, you might not survive the night."

He winks—that casual, daring wink that Toni is still wildly envious of —and says, "At least I'll die in the arms of a beautiful woman."

She blushes, but before she can come up with a retort of her own, a bald man with a brunette on his arm—who looks to be the man's wife, judging by the enormous size of the diamond on her wedding ring—strides up to Nicolas with a brilliant smile.

"Nico!" he booms. The two men shake hands, and then the bald man takes off in a long stream of rapid Spanish.

Toni settles in against Nicolas's side, holding his elbow lightly and surveying the crowd.

The rest of the night goes much like that. Nicolas cuts quite a popular figure. Folks come up to him again and again all night long to shake his hand, clap him on the back warmly, laugh with him and pay their dues. He handles it all with his standard effortless grace.

"Are you running for office?" Toni whispers to him at one point.

"I am merely being polite," he huffs back. To a man passing by, he says, "*Ciao,* Don, good to see you."

"The great and powerful Nicolas Perez! It is an honor to be here with you tonight, my friend."

"The honor is mine, Don. Go try the shrimp; they're fantastic." The men shake hands once more before Don shuffles off in search of whichever waiter is guarding the amuse-bouches.

When he's gone, Toni turns back to Nicolas. "Bend down for a sec. Let me see the top of your head."

He complies, though he frowns in confusion as she pokes around the hair on the top of his head. She can't help but run a few teasing fingers through the thickets of it. For a man pushing sixty, his hair shows no signs of vacating his scalp anytime soon.

"Are you checking on the status of the salt and pepper?" he inquires.

"No," Toni says. "Just seeing if you had a crown on up there."

He pushes her away, laughing. "I should've known better."

"You'll learn one day," she says.

"Yes," Nicolas replies. His eyes gleam with an unspoken intensity. "I hope to. One day." There's a bigger meaning to those simple words.

*One day.* A future together. Is that possible? Probable? Is it wise? As always, Toni has far more questions than answers.

Blushing, she hands Nicolas her clutch. "I'm going to go find the restroom. Do you mind holding this for me?"

He nods and takes it from her. "I'll be here when you return, *bella*."

Toni smiles faintly, then hitches up her dress and goes off in search of a bathroom.

She locks the door behind her when she finds one. It is a nice relief to step into a little oasis of silence. She checks her makeup in the mirror and rinses the stubborn crumbs of shrimp crostini off her fingertips.

Then, she pauses for a second and takes stock of her reflection. She hardly recognizes the woman looking back at her. Since when does Toni Benson look so—well, so much like *this*? There's a graceful, elegant, exotic woman gazing back at her. A woman who wields her age like a weapon, rather than hiding it like a blemish. A woman who is stronger for the things she has suffered through, not weakened by them.

Oh, how things have changed.

She unlocks the door and emerges back into the bubbling crowd. Nicolas, true to his word, is standing right where she left him.

"All is well?" he asks.

"All is perfect," Toni says.

Just then, a chord of music strikes, a bit louder than anything else thus far this evening. Nicolas glances up at it, then back down at Toni. "A little dance, perhaps?"

She pretends to weigh his offer for a long moment before smiling back. "Fine," she says, "but nothing fancy! Lord only knows how this dress will respond to one of your more outlandish flourishes."

"Don't tempt me," he says.

She stifles a laugh as they make their way to the space being cleared for a makeshift dance floor. As the music builds up and a handful of couples find the space, Nicolas takes Toni in his arms.

It's a slow song—decidedly not a tango—and Nicolas keeps his promise of nothing fancy. It's nothing much of anything, actually, more of a slow sway back and forth with their torsos pressed together than what Toni would call dancing.

But that's just fine with her. Nicolas's smell, his bulk, his warmth— those are the things that matter to Toni in this moment. He's gazing down at her with those liquid gray eyes and the hint of a smile playing at the corner of his lips.

"Stay with me," he says. It's a husky whisper, barely audible, and yet it sends an outsized chill skimming over the surface of her skin.

"What?" she whispers back.

"Stay with me. Here. Don't go back to America."

Toni's jaw falls open. She knows she ought to close it (her mother's voice in the back of her head is crowing, *"You'll catch a fly if you keep your mouth open like that!")* but hearing Nicolas implore her to stay in Argentina with him is...

Well, she was going to say that it was a shock. But is it?

Of all the frightening thoughts she's entertained over the last eight months in Buenos Aires, that might be the most intimidating of all.

Love is one thing. Love is malleable, adaptable.

But staying down here? That is a binary decision. Either she does it, or she does not—there is no compromising. It would mean so many things—giving up on the idea of Nantucket as her home; selling the inn; embarking on an adventure where all the rules have truly been tossed out the window, like jumping out of a plane with only faith instead of a parachute.

Is she ready for that?

*I don't know, I don't know, I don't know.* Her thoughts are a helplessly broken record.

Perhaps the wildest thing of all is how possible it all feels. She could say yes; she could stay. She could sell the inn and forgo the plane ticket home that has been sitting in the back of her head practically since the moment she left Nantucket.

She rests her cheek on Nicolas's chest. His heart beats steadily, comforting her like a mother's lullaby. Her eyes catch something in the crowd—a flash of silver hair, a dimpled smile, a teasing wink. Then it's gone.

But she could swear that it was her brother.

Her heart lurches again. It's in a permanent state of lurch these days, for reasons good, bad, and inexplicable.

Perhaps she's known for a long time, deep in her bones, that a moment like this might be coming. A decision point.

That is a terrifying proposition.

Doesn't it feel possible, though? Is she holding her future in her hands? Could this man—this frustrating, courteous, handsome, utterly unpredictable man—be what she has been missing for so long?

*I don't know, I don't know, I don't know.*

"I…"

"Say yes," Nicolas urges quietly. "Stay with me."

"I don't know."

"What is there not to know? I love you, Toni. I want you to stay with me. I want you to be with me."

Suddenly, this all feels like too much. Are the walls caving in? Is it hot? Why is her vision swimming and why are her hands trembling and why can't her lips and tongue form words to say what she wants to say: that she *does* want to stay with him; she's just so scared of severing all the threads that tie her to her past?

If she could just say that, he'd get it—she knows he would. *Say something*, she screams to herself internally. *Just say you're scared! He'll get it. You know he will.*

But she can't. Her lips won't work. The words keep getting stuck in her throat.

"Will you stay, Toni?" he presses again. There's almost a kind of gritty desperation in his face and voice now. He's pleading with her in a way that she knows must be tearing at the very definition of who he is as a man.

She was only partly joking about the crown—there is so much about Nicolas that is truly regal. So for him to beg her like this? It's unprecedented.

And shouldn't she understand that that means he wants this badly? That when he said he loved her, he really meant it?

Why can't she accept that?

*Why won't you let yourself be loved?*

Toni looks up into Nicolas's eyes. "Nantucket is my home," she says in a meek, trembling voice.

Nicolas blinks, taken aback. "What?"

"I...can't..."

"You don't live there anymore."

"It's my...It's home. I don't know. I don't know."

"You..." He blinks again.

And then Toni sees it, something she hasn't seen since the night she had drinks with Nicolas and they played that silly questions game together. She sees the shield slide back over his gaze. It hardens right before her eyes, and it's the most complete and subtle transformation she has ever seen in her life.

He isn't her Nicolas anymore.

He becomes, at the snap of her fingers, the man in the airport who thought she was a drunken idiot for questioning whose luggage he was holding.

Icy. Cold. Distant. Gone.

"You are stuck in the past," he snaps. "And you refuse to step a single toe into the future." He lets her hand drop. Then he steps away from her, leaving her on the dance floor.

Every inch of separation feels like a chasm that will never be crossed again. Every second without his touch feels like an ice age in and of itself.

Toni knows it at once—this is how it feels to truly be heartbroken.

# 15

The Fourth of July dawned bright and clear, a classically beautiful Nantucket day.

Toni felt miles better than she had when she woken up yesterday morning. No hangover to speak of, and she didn't let herself get railroaded into wallowing in her grief for the first thirty minutes of the day.

Which isn't to say that she sat bolt upright the second her eyes opened and started singing Disney songs to the birds outside her window, either. Not by a long shot. But given how she'd been feeling ever since she saw that pair of women's shoes in the front hallway of her home in Atlanta, she wasn't likely to complain about starting the day in a bit of a better mood.

That being said, it was hard to decide what she *ought to* be feeling. Was it wrong to be happy? How soon was too soon to move on? Should she be excited or fearful, grateful or miserable? Lots of questions with very little in the way of answers.

One decision that did seem relatively easy to make: Those were all problems for a future Toni. Right-here-and-now Toni didn't need to be worrying about any of them. For one day at least, she could just enjoy her home, her family, and perhaps a wine cooler or two, while they went down to the beach to celebrate with the rest of the folks gathered on the island for the day's festivities.

As was her custom, Mae was up before everybody, already elbow-deep in whipping up banana pancakes and bacon for breakfast.

"Good morning, sunshine!" her sister-in-law chirped as Toni came downstairs after a quick brush of the teeth and wash of the face. "How'd you sleep?"

"Like a log, a rock, and a baby all combined into one."

"Well, that's wonderful to hear! If only I were so lucky. I just can never get a good night's rest when Henry's gone."

Toni nodded sadly. "I do wish he was here. He better at least be catching some big fish."

"Knowing him, he's probably a few beers deep and shooting the breeze with the other wise guys while someone's poor nephew does all the hard work."

"That does sound frighteningly familiar. Speaking of someone doing all the hard work, let me help you with something. Can I set the table for breakfast?" Toni asked. She didn't wait for an answer, knowing that Mae was liable to balk. Scooping up handfuls of flatware and plates, she laid out spots for herself, Mae, and all the kids to eat together.

When that was done, she assembled a couple of canvas tote bags with beach supplies—towels, sunblock, snacks—and set them by the front door, along with Brent's toy wagon and an umbrella for them all to sit under.

The plan was to hang out at the beach for most of the day until the sun set, then watch the fireworks from their perch there. Despite the miles of beach available on the island, it could be quite hard for latecomers to find a good spot to view the show. Mae and Toni knew that it was better to hit the beach early and stake out some primo territory.

As long as all the kids were adequately fed and watered—and, just as importantly, the adults had sufficient supplies in the way of alcoholic beverages—today had all the makings of a glorious, relaxing day. Toni had a book in mind that she'd been meaning to get to forever. Maybe she'd finally crack it open. Or maybe she'd let Brent coax her into waging an impossible war between his sandcastles and the tides. There was no wrong option, really.

The kids came trundling down the stairs in short order once the smells of breakfast wafted up to them. Brent held Holly's hand like the little angel that he sometimes pretended to be, while Eliza did her best grumpy teen face and Sara strove to mimic it.

But by the time everyone sat down and was happily occupied with buttering and syruping their pancakes, it was smiles all around. Mae and Toni sipped their coffee—which they yet again declined to share with Sara—and nibbled.

"So, Mr. Brent," Toni said, "what are we building at the beach today?"

His eyes lit up at once. He didn't hesitate as he exclaimed through a chewy mouthful of pancake batter, "The biggest sandcastle ever ever ever!"

"Bigger than your dad?"

"Twice as big!"

"That's dumb. You can't even reach that high," Sara snapped a little peevishly.

Toni turned her sights to her sassy-beyond-her-years niece. "Well, why don't you help us out, then?"

"I'm going to lie out and tan," she said with a haughty tilt of the chin.

Toni hid a smile behind another gulp of delicious coffee. Sara wanted so badly to be grown up. It felt a little ironic, in the light of everything that had brought Toni here—all she wanted for herself was to go back to that age when the only thing that mattered was getting a tan like the cool older girls.

But there was no convincing Sara that adulthood maybe wasn't all she envisioned. And no point in trying, either. Toni remembered well how stubborn she'd been at that age, how desperately she'd wanted the same things that Sara wanted now. That was just life, and there was no way around it that Toni was aware of. The grass is always greener on the other side of the hill.

"And you girls?" Mae inquired of Holly and Eliza.

Eliza shrugged. "Gonna read my book. Then Suzanne and I are going to get ice cream downtown."

Holly said, "Mrs. Franklin said that it was okay with her if I hang out with them. Amy and I have a *lot* to talk about. She broke up with her boyfriend yesterday."

"Oh dear," Mae said with an amused smile. Toni chuckled along with her. She remembered that too—the ceaseless and all-consuming drama of thirteen-year-olds diving headfirst into the throes of young love. That part of girlhood, she did not miss at all. But it made her laugh to see how seriously Holly took it.

"So, can I go?"

"Yes, honey," Mae agreed, "but not the entire day, okay? And you need to be back with us for the fireworks. It gets to be a madhouse down there once it's dark out, and I don't want to have to go shaking down strangers to find my missing children. Besides, you're all much too good-looking to end up on the side of a milk carton, okay?"

"Yes, Mom," they all grumbled in unison.

After they'd all cleaned up from breakfast, they got changed into their swimsuits, gathered up the rest of the things they'd need for the day, and headed out to scout for the best spot.

There were already a decent number of folks out who had the same idea as the Bensons. But there was room aplenty yet to choose from, so Mae and Toni had no problem staking out a nice spread of sand on which to arrange their things and plunk an umbrella into the ground so they didn't get roasted alive by the day's hot sun.

From there, the rest of the day meandered to and fro like a gentle wave. Toni did a little bit of everything—drank wine coolers with Mae, built sandcastles with Brent, laid out alongside Sara and convinced her to divulge some of the burgeoning gossip that was occupying her tween brain. She even read a few pages of her book before succumbing to the kind of lazy nap that Nantucket summer days were specifically engineered to induce.

She woke up to a dying sun, feeling pleasantly crisped and blearily content with the state of the world. She licked her lips, tasted salt, and realized she hadn't thought about Jared even once since they'd set out from the house after breakfast. Small blessings, indeed.

Mae was just starting to get nervous when Holly and Eliza finally arrived back from their respective social obligations. Eliza was finishing off a delicious-looking ice-cream cone. Holly looked to be brooding over the day's latest episode of teen drama.

"Did you girls have a good day?" inquired Toni.

"Mhmm," was all Eliza had to offer. For her part, Holly didn't even respond. She just plunked down and looked preoccupied beyond her years. Toni chuckled and decided to leave her to it for the time being.

Soon enough, darkness had stolen over the sky. People had kept coming down the beach entrances in a steady stream throughout the day. Now, it was packed, with other families and groups verging in on all sides of the Bensons' patch of beach.

A murmur and the accompanying feeling of excitement raced through the crowd. There must've been some sign that the fireworks were beginning soon. As if they'd heard the news, the flow of new foot traffic to the beach seemed to double at once. It felt crowded all of a sudden, with folks swirling everywhere Toni looked.

Off to Toni's left, she saw Sara run up to Mae and poke her to get her attention. "Mom, I just saw Lindsay, and she said that her family has sparklers at their house! Can I go watch the fireworks with them?"

Mae shook her head. "No, honey. Stay here with us. It will be impossible to find each other in the dark."

"Oh come on! Please?"

"Darling, I said no."

Sara stamped a foot into the ground. "You never let me do anything! Whatever. I'm going anyway."

Mae started to say, "Sara, wait—"

But there was no stopping the headstrong girl as she turned tail and fled. She slipped between a pair of sunburned men and vanished into the crowd.

Toni turned to look at Mae at once. She could see the terror written in her sister-in-law's face. "Stay here with the kids," she said. "I'll go look for her. Don't worry."

Then she took off after Sara.

# 16

**THREE MONTHS LATER**

It is another cold, gray day in a long line of cold, gray days.

Lisbon in April is far more frigid than it has any right to be. The rain won't stop, nor will it fully commit to actually raining. It just keeps up at half flow, a perpetual drizzle that feels like someone ten stories up is spitting on Toni's head again and again.

"This isn't weather," she grumbles. She means that it isn't weather like they have in Nantucket. Back home, when it rains, it *rains*. When it snows, it *snows*. And when the sun shines, it really shines, and lights up the shores and the smiles of everyone lucky enough to be there.

This—this half-measure garbage—is irking her down to the core.

It makes the whole city feel damp and chilly and unfriendly. Which —not that Toni is much of a psychologist—is probably more of a comment on her own mental state than it is on Lisbon itself.

She knows why she's feeling the way she's feeling, like how a heavy drinker knows the thing that draws him to the bottle is the same thing that makes the drinking necessary in the first place. The poison becomes the cure awfully fast if you let it.

Toni's curse is the itch to fly from everything that has ever put her in the spotlight. She's done it again—she's run from Argentina just like she ran from Nantucket. But unlike Buenos Aires, Lisbon held no handsome stranger waiting to steal her luggage and sweep her off her feet. In fact, the terminal where she landed was strangely empty and quiet. More like a mausoleum than an airport. It gave her a weird sense of disquiet that hasn't left her in the three months she's been here.

Why here? Picking Lisbon wasn't the same sort of fortuitous lining-up-of-the-stars that accompanied her choice of Buenos Aires last year. She just needed to be gone, to be far from Nicolas—his hands, his eyes, his country. Crossing the ocean seemed like a safe first step.

So Lisbon it was. The wine was good here, or so they said, and that had been enough for Toni to buy the ticket and board the plane.

But the cheerful city of red-tiled roofs that the postcards promised didn't look so cheerful in the January grimness of her arrival. In fact, the whole place has looked downright unwelcoming. Windows stay shut up against the cold, and people hurry down the sidewalks without making eye contact.

So Toni does the same. She keeps her eyes down. She half-heartedly mumbles, "*Obrigado*" (which she learned was Portuguese for "thank you") to the servers at the restaurants where she eats or the grocery store where she buys her food. She doesn't dance. She doesn't drink wine. She mostly stays inside and reads books that don't bring her pleasure anymore.

And she tells herself that this is all part of her healing.

Even as she says it, she knows it is a lie. A shameful one at that, because she has stuck to it in spite of knowing that it is actively hurting her.

But what is her alternative? Go running back to Nicolas? To Camille? To Argentina?

No, she made her choice. She had the chance to say yes to all of those things, and instead she faltered at the crucial moment.

So maybe this isn't healing after all. Maybe this is punishment for her weaknesses. And if that's what it in fact is, then she has every intention of continuing to suffer until her penance has been paid.

Whenever that might be.

She told Nicolas that she didn't like being the center of attention. No one here pays a lick of attention to her, so she is getting her wish, isn't she? She is a nobody.

But then why isn't she feeling better? Why is she feeling worse than ever?

She knows the answers to these questions that are dogging her, which is a rare change of pace. Normally, she prefers to drive herself insane with questions that have no answers. These are easy, though.

She runs because she is afraid. And she is afraid because she is running. The poison is the cure, and the cure is the poison. Nothing heals. Nothing changes.

Three months of this have dragged by with agonizing slowness. How much more can she take?

Every time she comes in from the cold and swears that she is going to book a flight to Bora Bora the very next day, she loses her nerve for it at the last minute. Thankfully, the money from the inn has been steady enough to give her flexibility. She could go anywhere. Why not do just that? After all, Lisbon is a nowhere place, an awful place.

But she can't leave it.

Why not? Why not run from here? Of all places, why not escape this miserable dankness?

She doesn't know how to reason it out with herself. And when Camille calls every now and then to check up on her, she doesn't know how to explain that to her, either.

Toni trudges up the cobblestone road, full of switchbacks and patches of slippery sleet. Her hands are full of grocery bags, and her wrists have begun to ache from the effort.

Why she's chosen to stay in a small, cramped apartment at the top of the highest hill in the city is a mystery even to her. It is a twenty-minute hike just to get up or down.

Perhaps she likes it because, in spite of the misery of coming and going (or maybe because of it), she feels safe here. The remnants of São Jorge Castle encircle her ancient apartment building. A tall, thick wall of stone barring her from the outside world. The only things it lets in are tourists and rain. It is austere and beautiful and remote, and it makes her feel like she has sealed herself off in time and space alike. Nothing can touch her here. Not her past, not her future. It is like stepping out of the flow of history and living in a little bubble that is distinct and protected from everything else.

So when she finally mounts the hill and then the three flights of stairs to her apartment, she is stunned to find out that that bubble has been rudely popped.

The door to her apartment is slightly ajar. Her heart begins pounding a frenetic beat in her chest immediately. She sets the grocery bags down at her feet. The floorboards groan underneath their weight.

"He—Hello?" she stammers nervously. She pushes the door open. "João?"

João is the name of her landlord, whom she's seen maybe twice since she moved in here. He is an older man, dapper and stiff, who complains about every step from the ground floor up to the apartment. Dropping in on her unannounced—and letting himself into the apartment, no less—would be very out of character for him.

But she isn't sure who else would possibly be here.

A predator? Someone who has watched her comings and goings, who knows that she lives alone?

She has nothing in the way of weapons. Pulling her keys from her pocket, she tucks one between her knuckles like an old college roommate showed her years ago. She has no idea if it would do any damage whatsoever, or if she'll even have the nerve to swing at whoever is waiting inside, but it makes her feel maybe 1 percent better that she isn't quite so defenseless.

She pushes the door. It swings inward on whiny hinges. "Hello?" she calls again into the musty apartment. "Who is in here?"

Stepping through the doorway, she searches the corners of the small living room. No one.

Then—the squeak of footsteps.

Floorboards protesting under a heavy bulk.

The rustle of fabric.

A soft cough—deep, masculine.

And Nicolas rounds the corner from the kitchen.

He looks somber when they make eye contact, no hint of a smile anywhere near his face. Toni gasps and drops the keys, which clatter on the bare wooden floor. She claps both hands to her mouth in shock.

"Hello, Toni." His gray eyes are placid and still, like a frozen lake's surface. He keeps his hands folded together in front of him.

"Are you...are you real?" she asks quietly.

He chuckles. "Well, I certainly thought I was. Do I not look real?"

"You do. That's why I'm asking."

"I see." He nods. "Why wouldn't I be real?"

She gulps past a dense knot in her throat. "I just...I thought I might be dreaming or something. Or going crazy. I don't know."

Nicolas tilts his head to the side. "Crazy?"

"I...Never mind. What are you doing here, Nicolas? How did you get into my apartment? How did you know where I was?"

He rocks back on his heels as he clears his throat and mutters something.

"What?"

"I said, Camille told me where you were. And your landlord, João—"

"I know my landlord's name," Toni snaps. She is feeling a sudden lash of anger move through her.

"I told him...that I was surprising you."

"That feels apt."

"I'm glad you agree."

"No," she blurts, shaking her head. "We are not doing this. We are not just bantering like everything is normal, like you didn't just show up in my apartment like a burglar. This is not a happy little surprise. I almost stabbed you, you know!"

Nicolas glances down at the keys, sprawled sort of sadly on the floor where Toni dropped them. "Somehow, I think I would've been safe," he remarks dryly.

"No," Toni says again. "No, no, no. Go away. Go home. Leave me alone." Her voice is thick with unspent emotion, and it feels like she's been shaking her head from side to side forever.

She marches to the front door and holds it open.

"That is the exit."

"I see that."

"You're not exiting."

"No."

"Nicolas, you need to go."

He steps towards her. She backs away instinctively as if he really were a burglar with bad intentions.

It's a good thing she does that, too, because for a moment there, she got a whiff of his cologne, and it made her heart throb so painfully that she thought she might start spilling the tears she'd been holding back since the second he stepped out from her kitchen.

Back here is safe. Maintain distance from him. From everything he's brought with him—memories, baggage, roads not taken.

But there's only so far to back up. Her shoulder blades make contact with the wallpaper, and she knows that there is no more room to retreat.

Nicolas takes another tentative step towards her. He reaches out a cautious hand as if to stroke her cheek, but when she flinches, he drops it. Instead, he sticks his hand into the inner pocket of his jacket and withdraws something.

It's a bundle of envelopes tied together with twine. He offers it to her.

"What is this?"

"It's for you," he says simply.

She takes it, being careful not to let their fingertips touch. She has this unreasonable fear that if they make even the slightest bit of contact, she will dissolve into a puddle and never find her way back to normal ever again.

Taking it and undoing the string knot, she sees that the envelopes all have her name on them.

She looks up at Nicolas. "What are these?"

He doesn't blink or look away from her. "I wrote you a letter every day since you left, Toni. I didn't send a single one. But I wrote them, and I decided yesterday that I thought you should have them."

"What do they say?" she asks. Her voice is husky and trembling.

"The truth."

"What truth?"

He hesitates again, though his eyes don't lose an ounce of their intensity. Then, slowly, he moves towards her, crossing that invisible line that's the only thing holding Toni together. The last of her castle walls.

And this close, where she can smell him and feel his warmth and notice every little pockmark and scar and hair on his face—where she can touch him if she chooses to, where his eyes have so much depth, and his lips look pillowy-soft—this close is a danger she cannot run from. A spotlight she cannot escape.

He is looking at her as if she is the last person on earth.

"Open the letters, Toni," he says.

She looks down and does as he says because if she keeps looking in his face, then she will fully melt, and there is no telling what will happen after that. Nicolas stands silently across from her. She can tell that he wants to touch her badly, but she can't bear the thought of that yet.

So she tears open the first one and reads it.

*Dear Toni...*

She's crying by the time she's done. She lets it fall to the floor, a fluttering paper snowflake with elegant longhand on it, and opens the second.

*Dear Toni...*

This, too, floats downward and settles at her feet.

The third—*Dear Toni...*

*Dear Toni...*

*Dear Toni...*

Three months' worth of letters that talk about love and fear and forgiveness and hope and all the things that rattle Toni Benson down to her core. Three months' worth of letters talking about the things that frighten her. She's touched this hot stove before—she knows how badly it burned her hand, and that is why she has run.

But Nicolas has followed her, and he's given her these words, and now he's standing in front of her with eyes blazing and hands in his pockets, and there is only one more letter to read.

She opens it with trembling fingertips. This one is not like the others. Her name on the front is written in professional calligraphy, all swirling and intersecting like ironwork.

She withdraws a gleaming placard from inside it. *The father of the bride requests your presence at the wedding, to be held...*

It lists the details and the name of Nicolas's daughter and her fiancé.

She looks up at Nicolas now. Her face is a battlefield of spent tears, and she doesn't trust her voice to work properly.

But he must sense that, because he smiles—sort of a sad smile, almost melancholy, but with happiness in it too, or at least something that maybe could become happiness if it got the right amount of sunshine and rain—and finally does what he has so clearly wanted to do since the second he first conceived this harebrained plan.

He reaches out and touches Toni.

His fingertips on her neck are like ten points of fire. Her skin flushes beneath his touch, and she lets her eyes fall closed to hold back the few tears that haven't yet been spilled.

"Toni," he whispers in a deep rasp. "I meant it when I told you I loved you. And if you don't want to stay with me, I get that, and that's okay. I will learn to live with it. We are not defined by the things we have lost, remember?" His eyes flash with something like mirth. "But I couldn't bear losing you without trying at least once more. So that's why I'm here. To try again."

She doesn't know what to say. What is one supposed to say in a time like this? She opens her eyes and looks at him again. Her bottom lip is shaking, perilously close to bursting loose in big, wracking sobs.

It feels like the crescendo of a tango—far more emotion concentrated in one beautiful, agonizing note than there ought to be. How can one heart bear all this at once: Henry and Jared and the inn and running and Nantucket and Lisbon and Buenos Aires and her mother and Mae and Brent and Eliza and Holly and Sara?

A memory leaps into the forefront of her brain: a photograph that once hung on the wall of the home she shared with Jared. In it, she is walking her bicycle down the beach access towards the waves. The wind is tousling both her hair and the simple white dress she's wearing. A thick, white-daubed lighthouse looms in the background.

She used to think the Toni in that picture was heartbreaking lonely as she turned her back on everything and looked mournfully into the distance.

But maybe that was wrong. Maybe that Toni knew sunshine was still a ways away, but it was coming eventually. She just had to have the patience to make it there.

And maybe this is it. Maybe, saying yes to this gray-eyed businessman with the strong hands is her sunshine. Maybe she doesn't have to run from him, from it, from hope, from love. Maybe she can let him love her, and she can love him in return. Maybe it isn't too late in her life to do those things. Maybe she isn't broken. Maybe she won't be afraid anymore.

It's a lot of maybes.

But, as the letters float around her ankles in the soft, whispering breeze coming through the cracked-open window, the maybes feel solid and real and possible.

She reaches up and touches Nicolas's face. His stubble rasps underneath her fingertips.

"I'll come to the wedding," Toni says. The last of the tears finds its way down her cheeks, but that's okay. Everything is okay.

Nicolas smiles. "Good." He has a tear of his own glistening in the corner of his eye, like a precious diamond. She watches as it falls, dampens her thumb, and hangs there for a moment.

Then she steps closer into his embrace and rests her head on his chest. And together, they begin to sway back and forth. A slow, careful dance, one without steps or any discernible rhythm, but a dance nonetheless. It is warm in here, and it smells nice, and Toni feels safe.

She is still scared. She figures she will always be a little bit scared.

But that is the thing of it—as long as she is here, being scared isn't such a scary thing at all.

# 17

Toni felt like she was on the verge of a panic attack. People everywhere, a crush of them on all sides, slick with sweat and sunscreen and the fumbled drippings of beers knocked out of people's hands by the endless passersby.

And still no sight of Sara.

She called her niece's name as she pushed through and past and around people.

"Sara! Sara!"

Her voice didn't last long before she went hoarse. But the cacophony of partygoers drowned her out anyway, so it didn't much matter if she kept yelling or not.

She wondered how and why all this was happening. In an alternate universe, she was happily camped out under the umbrella next to Mae, watching as the first of the fireworks burst overhead.

But that universe was not this one. In this one, as that first firework loosed its crackle and boom over the cheering folks gathered shoulder to shoulder on the sand, she began to feel a creeping sense of desperation growing beneath her unease.

What if she didn't find Sara?

Despite her young age, the girl was bold and confident, and she would probably—*probably*—be fine. But the possibility that maybe she wouldn't be fine was lit up like a neon sign in the back of Toni's mind anyway, as she thought it must for all women of a certain age who feel responsible for young children.

A million hideous possibilities existed for a girl lost in a crowd, and Toni forcibly kept herself from entertaining any of them. The one time her resolve broke, she pictured Sara's smiling face on the side of a milk carton with "MISSING" plastered underneath in urgent letters (like Mae had joked about at breakfast), and she almost had to stop to be sick.

But somehow, she managed to shuffle that nightmare scenario off to the side and focus on the task at hand.

She zigzagged up and down the beach in the direction Sara had gone. She went from the soft sand at the foot of the hills, all the way down to the water's edge, splashing impatiently as she kept going.

"Sara! Sara! Sara!"

No sighting. No response.

A few people turned to look at her curiously. Her mood stuck out like a sore thumb. Everyone else was relaxed, laughing, well on their way to drunk. But with every step she took away from Mae and the rest of the Benson children, Toni felt more and more nervous. She felt lost. And not just lost physically. As she kept weaving higher and lower, she realized that the sunny mood with which she'd begun the day was a lie. She wasn't past her sadness, not by any stretch of the imagination.

For crying out loud, it was just three days ago that she'd discovered the supposed love of her life shacking up with someone else in the home they shared! And she thought she was doing better? Ha! Self-delusion, it turned out, was a joke with endless mileage.

But something else had happened in that short time span since fleeing Atlanta, too. Something that seemed—at first blush, at least—maybe a bit more promising.

It felt to her like her grief had sharpened up, if that made any sense whatsoever. It wasn't that same shapeless, all-consuming black cloud that it had seemed at first. It had a form, and now that it had a form, it could be dealt with. Maybe not defeated—not yet—but caged up? Yes, maybe. That might just be doable.

Toni wasn't sure whether to blame the sun or the long day or the not insubstantial number of wine coolers she'd consumed, but as she pondered the subject and her voice calling Sara's name grew ever more strident, those twin dilemmas—finding her niece and caging away her grief—seemed to merge into one, until it seemed to her that solving one would be the same as solving the other.

She needed to find Sara. That was the key, the simple, achievable task that would be the stand-in proxy for fixing everything else that seemed so utterly broken.

*Find Sara, and you'll find the answer for what's next.* That's what Toni told herself. It seemed, for the moment, if nothing else, to be a plausible thing.

By now, she'd gone at least three-quarters of a mile down the beach. She was slicked with sweat, some of it her own and some of it belonging to the strangers she'd had to push past.

She reasoned that there was no way Sara would've kept going this far. She must've turned up one of the beach walks and left. Now that Toni thought about it, she did remember Sara saying something about going to her friend's house.

In her mad dash after her niece, she'd assumed that Sara would be heading to her friend's spot on the beach first. But maybe that was wrong. Maybe Toni ought to be heading into the neighborhoods to scour front yards for any little blonde girls with attitude beyond their years.

With nothing else looking promising, she veered in that direction.

Sand eventually gave way to asphalt as she charted a course off the beach. Toni didn't stop or slow down, even if an outsized panic was gripping her chest ever tighter like a squeezing fist.

*Find Sara. Find what's next.*

She didn't know the friend Sara had mentioned, or else she would've probably known where the girl's house was. So she had to settle for walking right up to the edge of people's yards and scrutinizing faces.

She got more than one odd look, but she didn't have time to stop and explain. What would she tell people, anyway? Ask them if they'd seen any blonde girls with sparklers? That would identify about half of the people on the island on any given Fourth of July. It'd be like asking a school of fish if they'd seen the one with scales. No, it was better to just keep moving, not to bother with explanations. One of these yards would turn up Sara, sooner or later.

She began to feel more and more desperate as she found nothing, though. Whether each yard was empty or filled with people she didn't recognize, it didn't take too long for her to verify that none of them contained Sara. And with each successive failure, that fist of fear squeezed a little tighter.

The show had begun, so fireworks were bursting overhead in rapid succession now, each louder than the next.

*Boom*—red. *Boom*—blue. *Boom*—white like orchids, as loud as God clapping.

The hangover that Toni thought she'd shaken lurched back, proving that she was naive for thinking that she was one of those rare late-thirties women who didn't get the dreaded two-day hangovers. She felt churning nausea and the vicious stab of a headache behind her eyeballs.

And then, like the heavens parting and lighting up the chosen one, Toni rounded a corner and saw a gaggle of young girls sprinting in happy circles around a manicured front lawn.

In the middle of them, waving her sparkler like a wand, was Sara Benson.

Toni practically fell to her knees. Only twenty minutes or so had passed since she had left Mae behind. But it felt like lifetimes had gone by in that short interval.

Did finding Sara offer the victory over Toni's sadness and anger that she thought it would? It was hard to say for sure. But as she ran over, plucked Sara from the knot of girls, and squeezed her in a tight hug, she thought that maybe it had. That, maybe, as she held an invaluable piece of her family in her arms and the fireworks burst overhead, she had forced the grieving into a little box.

It wasn't gone, of course. It probably never would be. But as long as it had a shape, she could deal with it. She could confront it or step around it, or at the very least just *make something of it.* That felt like an essential step if she was to move on with her life.

The next step felt essential, too, although this one had nothing whatsoever to do with Sara. As she held her squirming niece, she looked over the girl's blonde head and saw something on the corner of the street, two lots down from the yard in which she was currently kneeling.

The thing she saw was a dilapidated house. The same one she'd seen on her late-night whiskey walk with Mae, as a matter of fact, with the same bright red FOR SALE sign stuck out front.

When she saw it, everything clicked into place.

Toni Benson knew what she was going to do next.

Sara didn't say much as she and Toni walked back to the family. She was equal parts chastened and angry. Toni could understand that.

She'd never been much of a believer in fate, but something about this whole episode had begun to nag at her. It felt—well, "biblical" didn't seem like the right word. But it felt like it had a purpose. Like there was a reason that Sara was the one who had chosen to jet off after chafing under her mother's rules.

Why Sara?

Toni glanced down at the girl walking next to her. Sara didn't look back, which Toni also understood. Eleven-year-old girls are forever balancing right on that precipice between needing authority figures and getting ready to renounce them.

The girl was strong-willed, though—there was no denying that. She'd gotten much of it from her father, Toni suspected. Henry was as stubborn a mule as had ever graced the face of the earth.

But there was more to Sara than stubbornness. Or at least, that's how it seemed to Toni just now. Guessing character traits in children as young as her niece was always a risky endeavor. At Sara's age, the things that would one day come to define their personality were just rough sketches, with the final lines not quite done up in pen just yet.

So, Toni didn't think it was fair to determine whether Sara would grow up to be plain obstinate or something a bit different. And yet, she felt certain that there was more than sheer "don't-tell-me-what-to-do"-ness bubbling up in the girl. There was a sense of something more substantial to her. A willingness to do whatever was necessary to seize the things she thought she deserved. Was there something to be gleaned from that?

"You shouldn't have left," Toni said.

Sara huffed and blew back a bang that had come loose over her forehead. She said nothing.

"Your mom was really worried."

"I'm fine. I know my way around. We've lived here forever. Everyone knows us."

"There are a lot of strangers here, Sara. You never know what kind of people are around."

Sara huffed again. "I'm fine."

It took a lot of willpower for Toni to keep herself from reaching out and tucking away Sara's unruly lock of hair. Just like with the fear of losing a child to something horrible that Toni suspected every woman retains deep in her bones, she felt this soul-deep urge to reach out and touch this fragile child to let her know that she was loved.

But at the same time, she knew that that was exactly the kind of gesture that would throw up a permanent roadblock between them. Sara didn't want to be consoled or fussed over. She wanted—well, that was a good question now, wasn't it?

What did Sara want?

What did Toni want?

What did *anyone* want?

The more she thought about it, the more she thought the question was long overdue. When was the last time Toni had asked herself what she wanted—not in relation to her husband or to her job or to her friends or family, but just that question, alone and untethered by the sense of obligation she felt pulsing in her temples all the time?

She'd spent a lifetime doing things for others, or because of others, or on behalf of others. But what did *she* want?

Toni stopped, turned, and knelt on the edge of a yard. She grabbed Sara's arms and made her stop to face her, too, even though she knew her niece wouldn't like to be pushed and pulled so.

But this was important.

"I want to say something, and I want you to think about it before you answer, okay, Sara?" Toni said. "And you don't have to tell your mom if you don't want to, because this is just a thing for me to say and you to hear, all right? Does that make sense?"

She feared that it wouldn't make sense or that Sara would be too irritated to take her psychotic aunt seriously.

But, thankfully, Sara tilted her head to the side and nodded with a solemn expression on her face. "Okay," she said.

"A lot of people like to tell other people what to do. And a lot of people think that they're supposed to listen to that, and just do whatever they're told. And you sort of just learn to live your life like that."

Toni swallowed, wondering if she was making some horrific parenting error that would require decades of therapy to fix. But it seemed so important that she get this message through to Sara, even if she herself didn't understand it yet.

"So what I want you to remember is this: You do what you want, okay? You should do it for the right reasons, and you should listen to other people and think about what they're telling you to do, and you should remember that your mom loves you very much and she wants what's best for you, so most of the time you should do what she tells you even if you don't understand it or don't like it. But at the end of the day, you have to be in charge of yourself, okay? It's really easy to give that up to other people. You do it without even realizing that you're doing it. And it's way harder to get back than it is to give away."

The fireworks show had reached its crescendo overhead, so her words were punctuated with the roaring *rat-a-tat-tat* of pyrotechnics exploding in the Nantucket night sky. They lit up Sara's face in alternating colors, sparkling in the irises of her eyes. She hadn't blinked once or looked away from Toni. And, though it could've just as well been her buzz making her think this, Toni felt that the things she was saying were sinking in somewhere deep in Sara, finding root like seeds that wouldn't bloom for years.

"Do you understand, Sara?"

Sara waited a long moment before she nodded. "I think so."

Toni nodded back. *Boom-boom-boom,* faster and faster went the fireworks until the final conflagration went up, and then silence stole over the island in its wake. The lights faded from Sara's eyes.

"You're crying, Aunt Toni," the girl said suddenly. Concern knotted in her voice.

Toni touched her cheeks and found them damp. "It's okay, honey," she whispered. "I'll be okay."

She wiped away her tears with the back of her hand and squeezed Sara's fingers tight in her hand.

"What do you want to do now?" she asked.

Sara thought about it. "Let's go back to Mom," she said.

Toni nodded, stood up, and then the two of them went back down the road and onto the beach, swimming upstream against the flowing crowd that had begun to disperse back to their hotels and vacation rentals.

Neither of them said much as they walked towards Mae's umbrella. The moon was full and bright. Toni admired how it lit up the foam that capped each wave. It looked ethereal and glowing, like something from another world.

They came up to the spot on the beach. Mae, Eliza, Holly, and Brent had packed everything away and stood waiting. As soon as Mae saw that it was Toni and Sara who were approaching them, she rushed over and scooped up Sara in her arms.

"Oh my goodness, honey—please don't ever do that again!"

Toni watched, saying nothing. Mae was such sweetness and light, maybe enough so that she had a difficult time seeing that Sara was made of grittier things. The two of them would have some tough years ahead, Toni predicted. She could see them butting heads even now.

But she felt a strange new kinship with her niece. It was a classic case of learning more from our children than we teach them, she thought. Wisdom from the mouth of babes—that sort of thing.

So when Mae finally set Sara down and switched gears from being grateful that she was safe, to being furious that she'd left in the first place, Toni caught Sara's eye. And she smiled—just once, quickly, maybe not even distinctly enough for the girl to notice the gesture.

She tried to say everything that she couldn't say to her niece just yet, the things she'd hinted at in her impromptu monologue. There was no telling whether it landed, whether she understood. She was still so young, after all, and there were many years of heartbreak and struggle ahead for a young woman.

But maybe she got it. Maybe she understood. Maybe it mattered.

～

Everyone was exhausted from the long day they'd had and the adrenaline dump of the fireworks show, so there was little conversation as they went back to the house. The kids dispersed immediately to shower and get ready for bed. Mae went in to empty the coolers of the remaining snacks and drinks, while Toni offered to drag the umbrella, chairs, and other things to the side yard to rinse off the sand with the hose.

She did her work quietly by the light of the security lamp affixed to the side of the house. After the cacophony of fireworks and crowds, it was nice to listen to little more than the chirp of insects and the gurgling of the hose.

When she'd finished, she stacked the things neatly so they could dry overnight. Then she walked back around to the front.

Mae was opening the door just as Toni mounted the porch steps. She had a curious look on her face.

"Everything okay?" Toni asked.

Mae wrinkled her nose. "You have a...phone call," she said carefully. "It's Jared."

Her words hung in the air like the last of the fireworks.

Never before had it been so clear to Toni that she was standing at a crossroads in her life. There was, of course, no telling what Jared would say to her if she took that call. The fact that he was calling at all would suggest that there was at least *something* left between them, some semblance of affection or caring that could maybe be resurrected if they worked at it hard enough.

But then there was the other choice: What if she didn't pick up? What if she just said, *No?* No to Jared, no to reconciling, no to all those thousands of crowding voices in her head that were constantly yelling at her to put what she wanted dead last and worry about everyone else first?

What if she was more like Sara?

Toni looked down at Mae's outstretched hand, holding the cordless phone to her like a baton. She took it gingerly, half afraid that it might explode if she jostled it too much.

Mae took one more searching glance at Toni's face before she offered a quick, tight smile—something like a pat on the shoulder—and ducked back inside to leave Toni alone on the porch.

Toni slid slowly into a rocking chair. She looked out at the night, then down at the phone in her hand. She heard a tinny voice call out, "Hello? Mae? Toni?"

Only three days had passed since she'd last heard Jared's voice, but it already felt so foreign. Had he always sounded so reedy and nasally? Had she merely convinced herself otherwise?

She felt like she was having an out-of-body experience—or rather, the exact opposite, more like an extremely in-body experience. She'd never been so aware of her breathing, of the flutter of her eyelids, the tingling of rising sunburn in her hands and feet. She felt so *here* that it hurt.

Then she reached out with her thumb and, without saying anything to the man on the other end of the line, she ended the call.

*Click.*

She let loose a long, heady sigh. She closed her eyes and pictured it again—the dilapidated house, the FOR SALE sign in front. She knew instinctively that she was picturing her future. She was going to do what *she* wanted, maybe for the first time ever.

Then she opened her eyes again and dialed the number seared into her mind's eye. No one answered, of course, given the late hour. But then the answering machine clicked on with its prerecorded message.

"Hello, you've reached Nantucket Realty Co. Please leave your name and number and we'll get back to you as soon as we can."

*Beep.* That breathy silence swallowed her up, like staring into a dark cave. She swallowed, but she faltered for only the briefest of moments before she spoke into it.

"Hi, my name is Toni Benson. I'd like to buy the property you have listed at..."

She rattled off her details and intentions, then hung up the phone. She stared out into the night once again.

It amazed her how all these little things had amassed into this big *thing,* this dream on the verge of becoming a reality. That feeling of a full house, the B&B that had shut down, Kendra and Andy's baby, the unexpected finding of the rundown property that Mae thought had good bones...It was like someone had laid out all these hidden things for her, and only now was she beginning to see the way they were meant to come together.

She was going to build an inn on Nantucket.

Toni Benson had never believed much in fate, but as she breathed quietly to herself and soaked in the clean, beautiful air of the island she loved, she knew one thing for sure: it felt right to be home again.

THE END

Thank you for reading *No Love Like Nantucket,* Book 4 in the Sweet Island Inn series! Next up, check out *Just South of Paradise,* the first book in my series of a heartbroken woman finding new life and meaning in the wake of divorce.

## JUST SOUTH OF PARADISE

**Georgia Baldwin is just south of paradise, and just shy of a happy ending. Can she find the love she's looking for?**

Georgia had the perfect life—until her husband of nearly forty years leaves her for their inn's much younger housekeeper.

Starting over at fifty-eight is a terrifying prospect. And that's not all.

Her oldest child, Melanie, is trying to pick up the pieces of her broken heart after a difficult break-up.

Georgia's other daughter, Tasha, left Willow Beach to make it in Hollywood, but she's having an awfully hard time coping with failure.

Golden child Drew thought he was headed for the baseball Hall of Fame. But when he's unexpectedly cut from his minor league team, he is forced to take a long, hard look in the mirror.

Running the Willow Beach Inn, helping her grown children navigate the choppy waters of life, and rediscovering her own passions is no easy feat. Is there hope for Georgia to find happiness in the wake of heartbreak?

*Taste the salt on the air and feel the warm love of the Baldwin family in Book One of the Willow Beach Inn series from heartwarming women's fiction author Grace Palmer.*

Click here to start reading.

**Sneak preview of *Just South of Paradise*...**

With one week until Memorial Day, Georgia Baldwin can feel the busy season just ahead of her like a tingle of electricity in the air. It makes her climb out of bed a little faster and adds a little spring to her step.

It's rare for the Willow Beach Inn—the bed-and-breakfast she and her husband own—to ever be empty. But the summertime period bookended between Memorial Day and Labor Day is inevitably guaranteed to be chock-a-block full. And that means there is lots of preparing to do.

Georgia wakes her husband Richard by gently prodding him as she brushes her teeth. He sleeps through any and every alarm, so a little jab in the ribs is often the only way to wake him in the morning. It's one of his favorite things to grumble about, but Georgia doesn't let that faze her. Besides, he gets her back whenever he gives her a playful pinch if she happens to bend over within arm's reach. Fair is fair, Georgia supposes. She's always thought that much of having a successful marriage comes down to deciding which of your partner's little peccadilloes to tolerate or learn to love.

"Good morning," she chirps to him, voice muffled by the toothbrush. "I'll see you downstairs in ten."

Richard groans and rolls over, but Georgia leaves him there. He'll get up sooner or later. They have been running the inn together for the past fifteen years and Richard has never shirked his duties.

Georgia heads downstairs to the living room of the owners' quarters, then through the swinging door into the kitchen. She flicks on the light, dons her apron, and takes a deep breath.

Of their six en-suite guest rooms, three are currently occupied. There is a lovely young newlywed couple in the Magnolia Suite, their most expensive ocean-view room that features its own sitting room. Mr. and Mrs. Kleinman are in room 2. They are regulars who have returned to the Willow Beach Inn every year for the past five years. They usually spend the week before Memorial Day here, which Georgia has always found quite odd since everything seems to happen in the weeks afterward, but the Kleinmans say they like Willow Beach best right before the crowds hit.

It's a sentiment Georgia can understand, even if she disagrees. Personally, her favorite time is the height of summer, when the inn is just as bustling as the beaches outside, and at all times of the day there is at least one person sitting on the breezy patio overlooking the ocean. When she has the time, Georgia likes to be that person.

Room 4 has been taken by a man around Georgia and Richard's age, Mr. Brunswick. He is attending a conference in Portland but would rather slog through the forty-five-minute commute every morning than stay in the big city—not that Portland, Maine, would be considered a big city by most people's standards. Georgia can't complain about Mr. Brunswick, though. He is quiet, respectful, and always complimentary about her breakfasts.

Speaking of which, Georgia has a lot of work to do.

She turns on the oven and starts grinding coffee beans, drinking in the fresh aroma as it fills the room. She procures the beans from a woman that Georgia's middle child, Tasha, was friends with in high school. The woman and her husband owns a roastery and coffee shop on Main Street that always has a line out the door during the summer. The coffee is truly top-notch, and the smell alone is intoxicating.

As soon as the coffee is on, Georgia pours the batter she made last night into a muffin tray. She pops it into the oven just as the first pot of coffee finishes brewing, which is when Richard makes his grand entrance into the kitchen.

"Good morning, honey," she greets him with a wry smile.

"Mornin'," he replies, still a touch surly as he pours two cups of coffee from the fresh batch. He adds milk to his and slides Georgia's black coffee across the kitchen island, towards where she is opening a pack of bacon.

Georgia glances up at the clock on the microwave. Beautiful—seven thirty on the dot and they are right on schedule. "Thank you," she says. "Did you—"

"Pick up the new tablecloths from Ginny's Fabrics?" Richard guesses with a wink. "Yes, and they're washed, ironed, and ready to go on the tables. I'll go get them now."

"You're a gem, you know that?" Georgia takes a sip of her coffee and smiles at her husband. "What would I do without you?"

"Haven't the foggiest," he says in a horrendous fake British accent, pulling a wooden cart over to the fridge. "But I know you'd be doing it on threadbare tablecloths."

Richard loads the cart and disappears into the breakfast room to put out juice, butter, jams, and all the other little breakfast sundries the guests might want. As he sets up the breakfast room, Georgia takes her coffee over to the window and takes a sip while watching the first few beachgoers plod across the sand. The day is gray and a little misty so far but it usually burns off by the early afternoon. She likes watching that happen, like the day is opening up its own curtains to the citizens of the town.

It's remarkable how a place like Willow Beach can change so much and yet still stay the same. In all the years that Georgia and Richard have lived here, they've seen restaurants and businesses come and go —mostly the former, thankfully. Families, too, arrive and grow and spread, and little by little, the town takes on a life and a momentum of its own.

But some things never change. There have always been cawing birds in the sky, and beautiful misty dawns, and the smell of salt on the air. Those are some of the things that keep her grounded here.

The timer rings for the muffins. Georgia gets back to work...

Click here to keep reading.

# A NOTE FROM THE AUTHOR

My dearest readers,

Another book in the Benson family saga is done! I cannot thank you enough for the love and care you have shown this story. *No Love Like Nantucket* would not exist without you.

I want to convey to you my deepest thanks for taking the time to read and share my work. It still amazes me that there are people out there who care about the stories I have to tell!

I hope that you and your loved ones are all happy and healthy in this crazy time. If I may, one piece of advice: as Toni learns in this book, the sun is always just around the corner. Love and home are what keeps us safe until the morning returns.

As for me, it's back to the writing chair to dive in once more. As always—thank you.

With love,

Grace Palmer

# JOIN MY MAILING LIST!

Click the link below to join my mailing list and receive updates, freebies, release announcements, and more!

JOIN HERE:

https://readerlinks.com/l/1060002

# ALSO BY GRACE PALMER

**Sweet Island Inn**

No Home Like Nantucket (Book 1)

No Beach Like Nantucket (Book 2)

No Wedding Like Nantucket (Book 3)

No Love Like Nantucket (Book 4)

**Willow Beach Inn**

Just South of Paradise (Book 1)

Just South of Perfect (Book 2)

Just South of Sunrise (Book 3)